NOT BROKEN

Visit us at www.boldstrokesbooks.com

NOT BROKEN

by
Lyn Hemphill

2021

NOT BROKEN

ISBN 13: 978-1-63555-869-2

THIS TRADE PAPERBACK ORIGINAL IS PUBLISHED BY
BOLD STROKES BOOKS, INC.
P.O. BOX 249
VALLEY FALLS, NY 12185

FIRST EDITION: MARCH 2021

CREDITS
EDITOR: BARBARA ANN WRIGHT
PRODUCTION DESIGN: STACIA SEAMAN
COVER DESIGN BY TAMMY SEIDICK

Acknowledgments

Thank you so much to Alixander, who gave me so much encouragement and helpful advice I could have cried reading it!

To the inspirations: to The Sirens Call, my social life for years; to B., who now has his own Nina; and to my Farmer Boy.

CHAPTER ONE

Last Summer

The bus squeaked as the doors closed behind Rose, the morning's rain hissing under the wheels as it pulled away. She adjusted her bag and walked down Cowley Road. The sky was a heavy grey, and the entire city felt full of people pressed down by the day. She kept her eyes on the pavement, high enough to avoid bumping into anyone, low enough that she wouldn't have to interact.

A chilly wind whipped down one of the alleys, and Rose gritted her teeth against the unseasonal cold, shoving her hands into her hoodie. She turned her head to untangle her earphone cables and walked straight into another pedestrian.

"Sorry," she mumbled, stepping to the side.

"Hey, no problem. Look, take a flyer and we're even," he said in a perky American accent.

She forced a fake smile and looked up at him. Oh, good Lord, he even looked American, all big white smile and perky cheerful annoying-ness. "Thanks," she said, taking the shiny paper, which was black and gold and just…trying too hard.

"You know, you look like you could use a night off."

"I have the night off," she deadpanned. "That's why I'm going home."

He laughed, which was not her intention at all. "Great. How about you come to our gig later, then?"

Rose sighed and looked at the flyer, turning it the right way up so she could read the writing. Why did she do that? She should have shot him down. He took her attempt at manners as an opening. "We're on at the O2 Academy, just over there," he said, his eager puppy face lighting up, his out-of-control afro flying wildly as he pointed.

She scrunched her nose. The thought of being jostled in a dingy club didn't appeal much, but then again, neither did going home alone. She'd only go to bed early, then wake up at three in the morning, unable to go back to sleep.

"C'mon, we're about to be signed to an indie label. They need to see we're popular. Please?" His face crinkled. Spaniel puppy, she decided.

"What kind of music?" she asked.

"Alternative rock. I think."

"You think?"

"Hey, do you know how hard it is to define your genre when you also have to be completely unique?"

Rose snorted, a smile creeping up on her.

"Hey, you smiled. Win. So how about it?"

"Eh, it's not really my thing."

"What is your thing? I'm sure we can take requests."

She arched an eyebrow. "You must be desperate. Fine. Tracy Chapman, 'Across the Lines.'"

He pursed his lips. "Ooh, don't know that one, but we do a mean 'Fast Car.'"

"Everyone does 'Fast Car,'" she said, rolling her eyes.

"Oh yeah, closet hipster, are we? Tell you what, we'll do 'Feeling Good' by Nina Simone, and I'll learn 'Across the Lines' for you next time."

"Next time?"

"We're that good." He smiled smugly.

Rose couldn't help laughing. "Fine," she said, shaking her head. "Let me go home and get changed. I stink of the labs."

"Smart and beautiful, I got knocked over by the right girl."

She rolled her eyes. "Ugh. You were doing so well up until then."

"I'll see you later, sunshine."

She shook her head, but the smile was still there, curling up one side of her lips as she crossed the road. She glanced back at him, all scrawny limbs and mad hair and enthusiasm. He was still looking over at her and waved like a total dork. She didn't wave back, just shook her head again.

She fished around in her pocket for her keys and shoved the red front door with her shoulder, taking a deep breath of stuffy air. Up the stairs to her flat, peeling the damp hoodie off as she went, cramming keys and phone and earphones in pockets, in her bag, under arms. She struggled with her key in the Yale lock, muttering and swearing as always until it clunked and swung inward, nearly knocking her off her feet.

She let out a long breath, dropping the thoughts and impatience and boredom of the day at the door, kicking off her shoes, hanging up her coat, dumping her bag, and running her finger along the photo of Mum and Dad as she slouched into the kitchenette to flick on the kettle.

A cup of tea steaming in her hands, she pushed the curtains aside and leaned against the cold glass, staring at the street below. She much preferred it from this angle, seeing the tops of people's heads, not having to look out of the corner of her eyes in case someone glanced back. The flow of pedestrians made a complicated pattern, like the algorithm was just out of reach, clearly there, but not quite obvious enough for her to spot the numbers underneath. She stared until her eyes unfocused at raincoats and umbrellas, hair damp and lank from the drizzle, bicycle helmets and the tops of cars, their wheels hushing over the damp tarmac.

The sky darkened as she stood and stared, mindless and at peace, empty. She watched the man with the puppy dog face handing out his flyers, dragging people into conversation, more people than should have been possible on a dreary June day after a long week at work, but then he'd even managed to get her to interact. Maybe he had mutant powers like a comic book hero. She snorted and drained the last of her tea. Pretty rubbish powers.

She tapped a fingernail against the black flyer. *Stare at the Sun, O2 Academy, 8 p.m., supported by Martin and the Blowflies.* Who the hell came up with these names anyway?

She considered dumping the flyer in the bin, cooking up a batch of pasta and pesto, and watching some rubbish reality show on the telly again. She thought of last week, watching celebrities she'd never heard of on quiz shows or people on the latest dating farce, caricatures of themselves trying to stand out any way they could, and she felt so exhausted, she could have curled up on the tile floor, leaned against the corner between the cupboards, and sat there staring at the opposite wall. It would have been just as entertaining.

She glanced up at the picture of her parents, happy and holding hands. Mum had her head tipped back, her uneven teeth bared in a belly laugh, her eyes crumpled shut behind her glasses. Dad was looking at her with the fondest smile, so proud at having made her laugh like that. Both of them had matching ugly glasses. Rose had always thought that made them look twenty years older than they were, like they'd picked up the wrong pair when they came to England, but she'd watched them choose the damn things at Specsavers, had begged them to choose something more fashionable. They'd laughed and bought the cheap plastic frames with the beige and brown tortoiseshell pattern and delighted in their daughter's exasperation. She smiled and missed them.

Maybe she could try, just one night. Maybe she could find something to make her laugh again.

Chapter Two

Stare at the Sun

The O2 was across the road, a short walk through the post-rain air at half past seven. She paid her ticket and shrugged out of her coat and into the dark room. Her trainers clicked every time she took a step, pulling off the sticky floor, and her lip curled.

The room was low roofed around the bar, rising over the little stage, and there were already a few groups gathering around the support band. Nowhere near enough to hide herself. This might have been a mistake.

She cursed herself for wearing short-shorts and big hoop earrings. Everyone else, male or female, was in skinny jeans and overlarge black T-shirts. She also noticed, with resignation and absolutely no surprise, that she was the only non-white person there.

But as she turned back, already considering her escape options, she was proven wrong. The scrawny guy came out of a black door to the side of the bar, followed by a group of people. All of them wore the skinny jeans uniform, except an enormous West African–looking guy. Rose figured he probably couldn't find skinny jeans to fit; he must have been at least six foot five in both directions.

Before Rose could decide what to do, Scrawny spotted her and ran to kiss her on the cheek. She felt her eyes widen, and pulled back slightly.

"You came," he squeaked. "Thank you. I wasn't sure if I'd scared you off."

"You do that a lot?"

"Do what?"

"Scare people off."

He laughed and didn't answer, probably assuming it had been a joke. "I'm Harley," he said instead.

"Rose."

"Nice."

"Is it?" She raised an eyebrow.

"Come and meet the others. God, I'm nervous."

He did look wired, unable to keep his fingers still. She followed him to the group and gave an awkward wave, trying to remember names as Harley introduced everyone.

"These are my bandmates." He gestured to a little white girl with enough facial piercings to threaten airport security. "Joss is the keyboardist, and Frank"—he pointed to the giant carrying beers over from the bar—"plays drums. I'm the guitarist and singer. This is Frank's sister, Eliza."

Rose shook hands with a tall slim black girl with long braids, tattoos, and a lip ring flashing as she smiled. By the time she'd shaken hands with the whole group, she couldn't remember if Alicia was a white girl with a mass of red curl or a black girl with a Nirvana T-shirt and whether the Japanese girl was Miho or Yuko.

"Oh, and here's Jamie and Max. Guys, this is Rose, come and say hi."

Rose turned and...

Well, she wasn't going to forget these.

One was a little blond and stocky for her tastes, though he had a great smile, cheeky and knowing. But the other guy, Max? *Wow.*

He was an inch or so taller than her, the ubiquitous black skinny jeans a hell of a lot more appealing on him than anyone else. His green button-up shirt had the sleeves half rolled up, showing off ropy muscles on his forearms that Rose just wanted to touch. Glossy black hair fell in messy waves over his face, and his eyes were crinkled up with mischief and humour.

This was definitely worth getting out of the house for.

"Hey," he said, and she firmly reminded herself that she was a grown woman and as such did not giggle when a hot guy spoke to her.

"Hey yourself," she said in an extremely suave and not at all smitten way. "I'm Rose."

"Max." He smiled, a surprisingly cute expression that curved brackets around his lips. "So, uh, how did you hear about the band?"

"Harley leafletted me outside earlier. Are they any good?"

He nodded firmly. "They're brilliant, if BlackBox don't sign them today, they're idiots."

She raised her eyebrows. "Wow, you're…passionate."

He shrugged and looked a little awkward. She hadn't expected that. She'd expected arrogance, her usual type, but the hint of shyness wasn't as irritating as normal. "I love music," he said as if he was admitting some kind of flaw. "And these guys are really great. I've been going to their gigs since they played the beer festival in Chelmscote. That's where I live. They were brilliant then, and they get better every gig. Seriously, you'll love it."

"Max, my love, stop flirting and have a beer," said Jamie, looping his massive bicep across Max's shoulder and kissing his cheek, and oh, wasn't that always the way? All the best ones were taken or gay. Or in this case, both. She sighed internally and sat on her disappointment, squashing it right back down under indifference. Oh well. They looked very happy together, Max leaning toward Jamie as if he was his rock. It was really quite sweet, and well, she still got the eye candy.

"Have you got a drink, darling?" Jamie asked, slurring slightly and cocking his head on one side. "God, sorry, I've forgotten your name already."

"You're a liability, James," Max said fondly.

"I really am, please remind me? It's terrible, I ought to be better by now but—"

"No problem," she said, shaking her head. "It's Rose."

"Of course it is, and where have you left the Doctor?"

She snorted. "Mate, if I'd found him, I wouldn't be leaving him anywhere."

Jamie's eyes widened in delight. "Yes! A woman of taste. You hear that, Maxie? Someone who appreciates David Tennant's...assets."

Rose couldn't help glancing at Max, thinking she'd let him be her doctor any day. Lanky white boys with dark hair were pretty much her taste.

"Max, could I borrow you a second?" Harley asked, appearing at Rose's side, his fingers tangling and twisting together. "There's a problem with the sound guy." He smiled at Rose. "Max can hear when the levels are out better than any sound engineer I've ever known. He'd make a killing if he wasn't so busy driving tractors with Jamie. Are you having a good time? Can I get you a drink?"

"Hadn't you better sort out your sound issue?" she asked, pointing at Max.

"Oh. Yeah, yes, sorry. Max?" He stopped twisting his fingers and started tangling them in his hair instead.

Max flashed Rose a quick smile and followed Harley

through the crowd. Rose figured there was no harm in watching him as long as she could.

Jamie had turned to lean on one of the posh-looking girls with a riot of stylishly messy curls, so Rose moved away. The room was nearly full by now, the forgettable support band had packed up and joined their own group of friends, and Rose shuffled closer to the bar, noticing that Stare at the Sun and their groupies no longer had the monopoly on diversity. There were even people not wearing skinny jeans.

"You all right? Fancy a drink?" The girl with the tattoos squeezed up next to her and paid for a couple of beers.

"So what do they sound like?" Rose asked, leaning close as they made their way back toward the rest of the group.

"I can't really describe it. Kind of electronic indie rock, but that makes it sound like Daft Punk. Harley's voice is just, I dunno, ethereal. But still powerful, you know? And Joss looks like a tramp, but she plays keyboard like freaking Mozart, and Francis…well, he's my little brother, but even I have to admit he's brilliant." She laughed at Rose's expression. "You'll have to wait and see."

"To be honest, I'm a bit intrigued. I've never seen a rock band with mostly black people."

Eliza scoffed. "You kidding me? Black people invented rock music. Look up Rosetta Thorpe, and then remember rock has its roots in blues and jazz. And don't forget Jimi Hendrix."

Rose laughed. "Yeah, I know, but these days. There's not a lot of diversity on that scene."

"Well, then. I guess they'll stand out. No bad thing in the music world."

"I'll drink to that."

Max was still fiddling about with the sound desk, bending over to talk to the guy behind the dials. Harley was standing next to him, biting his nails and twitching like a sewing machine, and Frank and Joss came up behind him, patting him on the back and nodding toward the stage. They started to strap guitars on, check the pedals and feeds and tap out a few truncated bars, looking over to Max every few minutes.

Rose noticed the crowd seemed to drift toward the front, acting all cool about it, but aiming for a spot near the band. Eliza threw the last of her drink back. "I hope you dance."

"Oh no. No, no, no, I don't know how to dance to rock music. All that pushing and shoving? I'm too pretty for that."

"Don't be stupid." Eliza laughed and grabbed her arm. "We don't mosh. It's not heavy metal. We just dance. Oh, and nobody cares what moves you're doing, it's not like a hip-hop joint where you have to have some sort of skill. Just throw your arms about."

"She's right, most of us can't dance if our lives depended on it," said Miho...or was it Yuko?

"Speak for yourself," laughed one of the other girls, and the group carried her like a wave to the front, 'scuse-me- and pardon-me-ing as they wriggled through the rest of the crowd, who were still playing it cool. "Hey, Hillary. Good to see you. Sophie, get your ass up here, they're about to start."

Rose stared at the huge group of people gathered at the front, chatting to each other, introducing themselves to strangers standing near them, or good-naturedly heckling the guys onstage who grinned back and flipped the bird at them.

All at once, Harley stepped up to the mic. "Evening, all. Having a good night?"

Eliza and the rest of the crowd whooped at them.

"Yeah, I know you lot are. Well, in case you wandered in by accident, we are Stare at the Sun, and this is what we do."

It wasn't what she was expecting at all. The group was tight, and their talent shone through. Frank alternately attacked and caressed the drumkit, smiling constantly, sweat flying. Joss let her hair obscure her face most of the time, and her eyes were closed whenever Rose saw them. Her fingers flew across the keyboard, and Rose could tell she'd had classical training.

But it was obvious that Harley was the main draw. She'd been expecting basic power chords being hammered out with enthusiasm to mask a lack of skill, and for some of the more upbeat songs, that was all it was. But when the tempo slowed, he'd play intricate arpeggios that chased the piano around until they caught each other and swirled in harmony. His voice was slightly nasal at times, which she usually hated, but it seemed to fit the songs, and he would often break through into a pure, soaring falsetto, perfectly on the note. She craved those downtempo numbers, wanting to stand and stare at the movement as they made the music that pulled her out of her body and made a puppet show of her emotions, but it was the faster, funky tunes that caught the rest of the crowd.

Eliza grabbed her and pulled her into an undefined half circle in front of the stage where their friends were dancing, all pulling in strangers from the fringes to join them. There really wasn't any skill involved, as Eliza had promised. Everyone threw arms and legs around in time to the beat, in some weird cross between a Charleston and the twist. Rose quickly noticed that you couldn't join in half-heartedly, and when she stopped feeling self-conscious and started making fun of herself, the rhythm found her feet, and she couldn't stop.

The dance was hilarious and exhausting, and when they played their last song, she was at once relieved and almost bereft, having to come back to real life. She joined the rest of the room calling for an encore.

"You want one more?" Harley yelled into the mic, face flushed and eyes gleaming with excitement.

"Yeah!" The room was now packed with fans.

"Well, I'm not so sure about that. I mean, it's past Joss's bedtime, look at the poor little thing."

"I'll tuck her in," yelled a boy's voice from the left.

"You've pulled, Joss." Harley turned his head to look at his bandmates, his hand on the mic, and his mouth pivoting round it so his volume didn't change. "Francis, have you got anything to say about that?"

Frank leaned down to his own mic. "Sorry, love, I'm not very good at sharing."

Joss winked at him, and Rose raised an eyebrow. "Are they really together or just working the crowd?" she asked, leaning toward Eliza.

"Yeah, they've been an item for years. Joss brought Francis into the band when she and Harley first started jamming together."

Harley was winding the crowd up again, milking it for all it was worth. "What's that? Ah, guys, my manager says we gotta go, the tour bus is on a meter. Next time though, huh?"

Everyone booed good-naturedly as he started taking his guitar strap off. "Shut up, you don't even have a manager."

"Or a tour bus."

Harley slapped his forehead. "I've just remembered. I promised a song to a beautiful girl."

Some obliging people, clearly fresh out of a pantomime, gave a lilting ooh, and Rose rolled her eyes. "Bribed me with it, you mean," she yelled.

"Semantics." He winked at her, and Joss started tapping out a simple blues rhythm, building its density as Harley and Frank joined in until Harley let go of his strings, gripped the mic in both hands and poured out his heart. The steady, powerful pace, even without the distinctive brass, swept over Rose, and she felt for a moment like a legion marched beside her as she dragged herself through the mud and grief into the promise of dragonflies and spring on the other side.

By the second verse, she knew they'd won. She'd be going to the next gig.

CHAPTER THREE

Sunbirds

She hadn't felt like this since university, writing down gig dates on her calendar, texting people, meeting up, and lift sharing. Possibly since before uni, where nights out had been much more spontaneous and certainly closer to home. For years, her only social life had been a weekly karate lesson, and it wasn't as if she spoke to any of those guys outside of sparring. Now, with the band, she was prepared to drive a group of people up to Coventry on a Friday night just to dance for a couple of hours to a style of music she never knew she'd liked.

To start with, Harley's voice had been the main draw, but as Rose went to more and more gigs, the entire atmosphere and the group of friends became essential. The social life she'd hardly noticed she'd been missing was all wrapped up in a neat little package of talking on long car journeys, dancing, drinking, and little spikes of drama to liven it up.

And of course, the music. She'd gone to very few live music venues in her life, and now she was watching the band and learning how they set up the equipment, what all the pedals could do for the sound of a guitar, and why Harley needed to change instruments so often. And then there were all the other gigs they caught at the same time, indie, electronic, metal, hip-hop, pop and grime artists who played the same gigs and showcases as Stare at the Sun.

It didn't hurt that Max and Joss listened to them all avidly, and Rose often stood beside them as they pointed out mistakes she'd never have heard and skillful handling of hard parts. Joss would often go up to bands and give them feedback. Some of them even took it well. Max preferred to stay in the shadows and soak it all up.

The names she'd thought she'd never learn now came as easily as her own. Miho, the Japanese girl with glasses who managed to be surprisingly not annoying for someone so sweet and good. The posh girls, Alicia with red hair and Chelsea with blond. Chelsea wasn't even her real name; she looked so much like someone off *Made in Chelsea* that nobody even knew what she'd been christened. Aretha, named after the Queen of Soul herself, but who'd rather listen to Nirvana, and Connor, who always wore his dog tags and twisted them between his fingers when he wasn't talking.

And then there was Max. And his boyfriend, of course. Jamie was good fun, made her laugh until her stomach ached. Was she jealous that he got a lot more of Max than she ever would? Sure, but she was a big girl. She could cope.

She stumbled through the door of the pub, wiping tears away and leaning on Miho's shoulder as Jamie finished his story of an old farmer digging a fuel thief's car into a ditch and then pretending he hadn't seen it, and what was the bloke doing walking around with rubber tubes and jerry cans anyway?

"Rose, you came, hey," Harley said, pulling her into a kiss on each cheek. "Hi, guys."

"Don't I get a kiss?" Jamie asked, grabbing Harley around the waist and swinging him around. Harley blushed furiously and gave him a quick peck on the cheek.

"Can I get you a drink?" Harley asked Rose as they walked into the bar.

"Oh, thanks. Just a Coke please, I'm driving."

"Responsible," he said with a smile.

She raised her eyebrows and shrugged. "Just taking turns."

He carried on smiling as if she was some sort of wonder, and Rose couldn't help shaking her head and smiling back. The boy was as soft as butter. "You all set up?"

"Yeah, we got here about half an hour ago and had a sound check. You can always catch a lift with me and the guys if you don't mind being here early."

"Why are you so keen to get me drunk?"

"Oh, no, nothing like—"

"I'm taking the piss, Harley, don't worry." She laughed and patted him on the arm. He blushed again, his skin not nearly dark enough to hide it. "Let's catch up with the others."

The crowd of hyper groupies, or Sunbirds, as Jamie insisted on calling them, opened to absorb them, thumping Harley on the back as he passed. Rose slipped into a thick, battered sofa next to Miho, who smiled up at her. Honestly, Miho and Harley were cut from the same cloth. They should have gotten together and had sweet vanilla sex.

There were times Rose would stop in the middle of a work day, thinking back to Miho's wide-eyed innocence and wondering what the hell she was doing. She was nothing like them. They were usually the kind of people she'd avoid like the plague, but she liked them, Miho in particular. Unlike every other "nice" person she'd ever met, she wanted to protect Miho and make sure nobody snapped at her the way she would probably do to any other "nice" person. She could even stand Harley, though she was more prepared to tease him. He seemed not to mind it, anyway.

Max was leaning over Jamie to talk to Aretha on the other sofa, his elbow digging into Jamie's thigh. His plaid shirt had slipped low, and she could see the dip of his collarbone and a tight undershirt beneath. Jamie tugged it up Max's shoulder, his smile strained, and Rose shook herself. She hadn't realised her staring had been so obvious.

So Jamie had a jealous streak. She wished she could tell him that he didn't have anything to worry about. Rose wasn't interested in being the one on the side, but people were weird. If he was going home with Jamie, what did it matter how much Rose looked?

The band started plugging their kit in and strumming, and the Sunbirds gathered their drinks and coats and stood, creeping closer to the little stage. The roof was low, and with the walls painted a dingy dark blue, it was a bit like being in a cave.

"Evening, everyone," said Harley, glancing around the crowd with a smile building as he saw how full the room was. "We are Stare at the Sun, and this is what we do."

They dived straight in to "Rectify," and Rose whooped as Eliza grabbed her hands, pulling her forward to bounce up and down to a ska-like beat. Miho spun Chelsea around, and Max and Jamie bounced up and down like lager lads at a football stadium, yelling the lyrics and spilling their beers. Rose threw back her head and felt at home.

❖

"You did amazing, Harley," Miho yelled as they came offstage, sweating and breathing hard. She squeezed him tight around the ribs, and Rose was amused to see her close her eyes as she pressed her cheek against his chest.

Harley smiled down at her and patted her head. "Thanks, Miho."

"You learned 'Across the Lines,' too. Finally, some good music," Rose teased, thumping him on the arm.

He leaned in for a kiss anyway. "What did you think?"

"You know I think your voice is brilliant, Harley. I want to hear you play that on Radio One Live Lounge one day, you hear?"

"I will," he said, and he sounded a lot more serious than he needed to, as if this was a promise he'd keep no matter how long it took.

She blinked and looked away, focusing on the group gathered by the bar. Strangers came up to the band, and Eliza sold EPs and badges and signed more people up to the mailing list. Connor was bending down to listen to Alicia, his arm shooting out and grabbing her waist as she stumbled, tipsy. Max and Jamie were still dancing, hands linked and throwing their feet out to "Footloose" like idiots.

"Here, Rose, have a drink," Miho said, pushing her way over and handing her a beer.

"I'm driving," she said, crossing her arms.

"Oh, go on, you'll be well below the limit. You know it's only, like, four percent or something. Wouldn't even register on a breathalyzer."

"No," she snapped.

Miho's eyebrows shot up, and her head actually swayed backward a little with surprise. Rose looked away. Miho nudged Aretha's arm and handed the beer to her instead. "Rose, I'm sorry."

"Forget it."

"No, I shouldn't…I mean, we're not in school anymore," she said, laughing, clearly embarrassed. "I should have grown out of peer pressuring people to drink, huh?"

Rose gritted her teeth. "It's really fine, I'm sorry I snapped."

Miho rubbed her bicep and smiled, the flickering lights from over the stage catching in her glasses.

Rose didn't know what made it come out. She'd never

really spoken about it before. Even in uni, her friends had known. Some had even come to the funeral. But she'd never spoken about it. "My parents got hit by a drunk driver."

"Oh, Rose, I'm so sorry. God, how insensitive of me. Are you okay?"

"Yeah, of course, don't be daft. It was years ago."

Miho looked up at her with big sad eyes. "Even so. Do you want to talk about it?"

"God no."

"Okay, well…if you ever do."

If she ever wanted to talk about it, she'd probably have had a personality transplant. But she smiled at Miho anyway with half her mouth and tugged her into a rough sort of hug, one-armed. "Come on, let's go join those idiot boys and dance."

Chapter Four

On Tour

"You? You're taking a week off at a time? You, Rose Pereira?" Andrea held her hand to Rose's forehead, and she brushed it off irritably. "Are you sure you're not coming down with something?"

"What are you on about? I take holidays."

"Only when Helen makes you."

"Stupid working regs. If I don't want or need time off, I should be allowed to get more overtime." She shrugged. "Anyway, I've never had a reason to want the time off."

"Oh," Andrea said, her eyes gleaming as she sat on Rose's stool and tucked her black hair behind her ear. "What's your reason?"

"Get your hair tied up, you scruffy urchin. You'll contaminate my samples."

"I'm nowhere near your samples, now spill."

Rose rolled her eyes and popped another pipette tip into the bin. "The band's going on a mini tour. We're going with them."

"No way." She laughed, sitting up straight. "Like in *Almost Famous*?"

"Huh?"

"Are you kidding me?" She squealed. "You've never seen *Almost Famous*? Right, that's it, movie night at mine. David, Lily, you're free tonight, right?"

"Well, I—"

"Good, bring crisps."

"Stop being so damn bossy, Andrea," Lily said. "Your gel timer's been going off for ages."

"Damn it. I've already run those three times. I'm going to run out of sample."

"Well, don't leave them going for so long, then."

"I'm just following the *pro forma*. What about you and your restriction enzymes? Any of them actually work this time?"

Rose grinned as her colleagues bickered and sent a message to the group chat.

Got my holiday dates confirmed. We're on!

Replies came thick and fast from the band and the Sunbirds. Miho sent a squee that ran for three lines, and Frank and Eliza both sent a string of emojis at almost the same time.

❖

Rose was waiting in the Argos car park for almost half an hour before the hired minibus pulled up for her, but she was so hyper, she didn't even notice the cold. The Sunbirds leaned out their windows when they saw her, whoops and juvenile shouts cutting the cold morning air. She grinned and pulled herself aboard, and they were off to the next stop.

Max and Chelsea were the last to be collected, sharing a ciggie by the side of the road near a McDonald's. Eliza honked at them and parked up. "All right, you've got half an hour to get what you want. Any longer and I'm leaving you here."

"Yes, Mum," Rose said, following Miho off the bus and winking at Eliza.

"Yeah, yeah," Eliza replied, rolling her eyes. She leaned

forward as another horn sounded. "Late as always," she yelled as the band's van pulled up beside them.

Frank had traded in his Focus for the Beast the moment they'd got the BlackBox contract signed, and within days, he and Joss had sharpied their logo on the sliding doors. They'd then added the dates and venues of every gig they'd played, and Rose was starting to wonder whether the DVLA would even consider it a white van anymore.

Eliza was dead serious about the timing and the rest of her new official status as band manager. As people returned to the minibus, she ticked them off a register and passed around copies of the itinerary. Alicia shoved a clump of red hair behind her ears and flicked through it. "Jesus, Lize, you've forgotten to schedule time for us to take a dump."

"Shit on your own time, princess. If I'm going to get those dopey-arse boys around seven venues in seven days, I'm going to have to be this stupidly organised."

Connor laughed. "Bloody hell, it's like being on deployment again." He clicked his heels together and saluted. "Sir, yes, sir."

"Get in, you pillock."

The first leg, down to Cornwall, was one of the longer trips, and half the group was asleep before they'd even left Oxfordshire. Rose leaned back into her corner seat and chatted quietly to Miho, watching as she applied perfect eyeliner in between speed bumps and roundabouts.

Max was sitting on Miho's other side, and Rose told herself she wasn't a teenager anymore, and she certainly wasn't allowed to get butterflies about her gay, attached friend. But damn, his legs went on forever.

"No Jamie this week?" she asked.

Max turned his slow smile on her. "Nah, October's not that

busy, but there's still quite a lot of ploughing and cultivation to do."

"You guys are farmers, right?"

"Contractors, yeah."

She raised an eyebrow, gesturing for more information.

"We've only got a small farm but a lot of equipment, so people hire us to do the farming for them. That way, a little farm doesn't have to get all the expensive equipment all the time, they don't have to worry about maintenance costs, and so on. We've got about six or seven farms on the books, but Jamie's dad is sending a bit more work our way now he's getting a bit older."

She nodded. "How come you're not doing something with music, though? You're crazy about it, and you're really good."

He laughed and looked down almost shyly. "Ah, no way. I can't play music. I just like it."

"You could be a sound tech, though," Miho said, putting her mascara away.

He scrunched his nose up. "There's not much money in it, is there? I know I've got a steady income this way and somewhere to live, at least. And I enjoy farming, really. I get to be out in the countryside, and I can listen to music all the time, too."

Rose shrugged and let it go.

❖

Miles of tarmac and countryside disappeared under their wheels, broken by overpriced service station food, uncomfortable sleep against the juddering glass, and conversations with a steady rotation of friends. It didn't matter who was sitting next to her, Rose felt like she could get along with any of these charming idiots, and her introversion sank away in the face of music and ratty hostels, long bus journeys and late nights.

She hardly spoke to the guys at the centre of the circus for days at a time, but when their little group of misfits gathered in front of a stage and the first chords split the night, they melded together to form an army. It was the music weaving them into a coherent whole that seemed to grow each night as more and more strangers joined their ridiculous dances, clapped in rhythm, and sang the words right back to the stage.

❖

Max started giggling to himself somewhere between Penzance and St Ives. It was only nine a.m. after another late gig last night, and even sitting next to him, Rose was starting to space out. She turned to him and raised her sunglasses.

"What are you sniggering at?"

He pointed at the car beside them on the motorway. "Their number plate says FML."

Rose snorted. "Damn. Do you think they bought it just for that?"

"I mean, I would."

She leaned on his shoulder to look over at the next car in the queue. "That one's DMZ." She sat back and scrunched her face up. "Department of Magical Zoology."

"All right, Newt Scamander." He smirked. "What about KTW?"

"What's with all these number plates and their high scrabble ratings?" she grumbled.

Max tipped his head back, tapping his chin. "KTW...Kill the Wicked."

"Damn, boy, start a band with that name. I was thinking more like Kittens that Wrestle."

Max laughed, his face crinkling up. Rose grinned and squashed that stupid fluttering in her stomach. The bus rolled forward a bit, shifting them farther up the line. "There, SJA," Max said, pointing at a little Vauxhall.

"Hmm. Sounds Just Awful," Rose said.

Max tipped his head back, and Rose bit her lip, watching his throat move. She tore her eyes away. *Not cool.* Jamie wasn't here to get jealous. But *damn.*

"Are you casting aspersions on that support group last night?" Max said, twinkling down at her.

"Would I do such a thing?"

"Absolutely, you would."

She nodded. "You're right, they were terrible."

"Suzie Juices Apples," Max said, snapping his fingers.

"That's so lame." She snorted. "Someone Juggles Arses."

Max almost doubled up with giggles. "How does someone juggle arses? You think I'm lame? At least I make sense."

Miho yawned and stretched in the seat in front of them, knelt on her chair, and blinked at the two of them, her chin resting on the seat. "What are you two doing?" she asked.

Max pointed at another car in the queue. "The reg-plate of that car is JCQ, any ideas what that can stand for?"

"Just Crap at Queuing," Rose said.

Max grinned. "Jason Can't Quit."

Miho blinked at them. "Uh, I dunno, Jenny Can...No fair, you guys took all the Q words."

"Queen," Rose said, smirking. "Quidditch. Question. Quoits."

"Quoits?" Max laughed. He looked fantastic laughing. Rose decided to keep him in that state of giddy hysteria as long as possible. "How does a townie even know about quoits?"

"I didn't know it was a country boy thing," she said.

"It's a pub game, like Aunt Sally."

"What the hell is Aunt Sally?"

He grinned. "It's a pub game. Like quoits."

Rose pinched her lips together and slapped him with the back of her hand. He yelped and pushed her away. "Don't you dare," she yelled, holding herself up on Chelsea's seat across the aisle. Chelsea blinked at her, then slumped back against Aretha.

Max grabbed her sleeve and pulled her back to the window again. "Oh my God, Rose...Rose, look," he whisper-shouted, pointing out at the car pulling past them. "It's the holy grail, Rose."

"SMD," Rose said, a gleeful smile spreading across her face. "Holy cow."

"What?" Miho said, leaning over. "What is it? I don't get it."

Rose snickered. "SMD...Suck My D—"

Max slapped a hand over her mouth. "Don't you dare. Not Miho, she's too pure."

Miho's forehead crinkled into a pout. "What?" she whined. "I don't get it."

Max and Rose collapsed in childish giggles. Rose could almost imagine she wasn't internally freaking out about him leaning his forehead against her shoulder as they cackled.

Miho groaned and sat back down. "You two are weirdos."

❖

"He likes you, you know."

Rose, who'd been staring at Max's slim waist and narrow hips trapped in tight black jeans, jumped guiltily. "What? Who?"

Miho sat next to her, holding out a pink cocktail and rolling her eyes. "Yeah, right, like you haven't noticed him staring."

"Really haven't."

Miho gaped at her, open-mouthed. "You're serious? You really haven't noticed the puppy dog eyes? Dude, I think Harley's had a crush on you since the day you came to that Oxford gig."

"*Harley?*" Rose turned in her seat to look for him, scrunching her face up. "Shut up, that's months. Why hasn't he said anything?"

She snorted into her mai tai. "Would you? Do you usually go up to people you fancy and ask them out before you know you're interested?"

"Uh, yeah," she replied. As long as they're not gay, she added to herself.

"Wow, you're, like, the most confident woman I've ever met. But most people aren't like that. Harley, for example. I think he's shy."

Rose snorted. "I think he's lazy."

"Harsh."

"He's not shy. You've seen him onstage."

"That's just a persona. The real Harley's nothing like that."

Rose raised one eyebrow. "You like him, don't you? Why are you trying to set us up, then?"

Miho sighed so the liquid in her glass fluttered. "What's the point? He likes you, not me."

"I really don't see how you can tell."

"I kissed him once."

"Oh, now we're talking. You go, girl." Rose affected an American accent and held her hand up for a high five. Miho met it reluctantly.

"Yeah, not so much. He didn't kiss me back. Said he valued our friendship too much, which, as everyone knows, is code for—"

"He's not interested." Rose nodded. "Damn. That sucks, but at least you know, and you can move on, right? Better than wasting your time pining."

Miho looked at her through narrowed eyes. "Really? You think I can turn this off?"

"Oh, I'm…really? You're still crushing on him? How long?"

"Coupla years." She shrugged.

"Bloody hell, Miho."

"So what are you gonna do?"

"About what?"

Miho rolled her eyes. "Oh my God, woman. Harley. Now you know he fancies you, what are you going to do about it?"

"Are you serious? You just about told me you're in love with the guy, and now you're back to setting us up? Of course I'm not going near the guy you've got a two-year crush on."

"Aw, don't be like that, Rose." Miho sat forward and grabbed her shoulder. "I said already, he doesn't like me, I'm no dog-in-the-manger. I'd rather see him with someone he likes than force everyone else away on the off chance he'll run out of options and get together with me out of pity. I'm pathetic, but I'm not there yet."

Rose frowned. "You're not pathetic."

"Sure, sure. So are you going to date him?"

She huffed a laugh. "I mean, Miho, he's not really my type. I wouldn't kick him out of bed, or anything, but I'm not…" She couldn't help glancing at Max dancing in a group with Chelsea, Connor, and Aretha, his hips swaying, and sweat glistening on his temples. "Yeah, he's nice, but…"

Miho looked amazed. "I thought you fancied him, too."

She smirked. "Seriously, just because you think he's the prettiest boy in the room doesn't mean everyone else does." She nudged her with an elbow. "He does have a very nice smile. And that ass. Yeah, he's cute, I'll give you that. But enough of this matchmaking, Emma Woodhouse. I'll buy you another drink."

Chapter Five

Misconceptions

By the time they were back in Oxford a week later, sweaty and cramped from travel and overtired to the point of hysteria, Rose felt like she'd known the Sunbirds for her entire life. It felt strange to return to work and have to think of things that weren't gig times and bunk beds. It was strange to go grocery shopping rather than argue about who was going to get takeaway or whether they were all going to subsist on beer and crisps and a late-night kebab instead. So when Eliza texted another three nights of gigs, scattered over the following few weeks, it felt only right to jump straight in with, *see you there*, and locations copied to her calendar.

Rose flicked back through the older pages, before the summer, how empty they'd been. One month, the only thing she'd marked was the start of *Game of Thrones*, and now she couldn't even remember if she'd watched it. She probably had, but it felt silly now, such a pointless thing to look forward to.

It had felt pretty pointless back then, too.

Rose glared at the calendar for daring to make her uncomfortable. She flicked back to October and checked her phone instead.

The Sunbirds kept in contact over the group chat, bantering and offering lifts, and it was Miho who picked Rose up for the next gig, Chelsea and Alicia squeezed in the back of her ridiculous old Ford Ka. "Hey there, stranger."

"I know, it's been all of ten days. How did we cope without living in each other's pockets?" Rose grinned.

The trip to Reading took longer than it should have, and by the time they arrived, Miho with her shoulders tensed up to her ears after the traffic, the guys were already starting to play. Max waved them over and smiled his slow smile, and Rose bit her lip and berated Mother Nature for making him gay.

Jamie was out in the crowd already, dancing with Connor and Aretha, bouncing up and down and shouting out the lyrics to "Don't Understand."

"You not dancing tonight?" Rose asked, leaning over so she could feel the warmth of Max's skin on her arm.

He shook his head. "Nah, I pulled something at work." He rubbed his ribs, his arms crossed firmly over his chest.

She winced sympathetically. "Bad luck. Did you pick up something heavy? You know you're supposed to bend your knees when you do that."

"That's back injuries, smartass."

She laughed and nudged him. He smiled, green eyes flashing under his lashes, but hunched his shoulders a little more.

She frowned and twisted her lips. She didn't think she'd been doing anything that could have made him uncomfortable, but he didn't seem to want to be around her. Fine. She could take a hint. She flashed him a smile, put her armor back on and joined the wild dancing while he hunched in the corner. She told herself she wasn't worried about him. He was being weird.

The lights spun and whirled as Stare at the Sun transitioned from song to song. Rose felt her skin heat, her hairline dripping with sweat as she threw her arms around and kicked up her heels, head thrown this way and that in abandon, the music sinking into her bones and moving her. When the tempo slowed, she slumped against Connor and Miho, linking arms with them and laughing, panting, singing along with their slowest song.

"Fire dust and sapphire skies, cold nights and heaven in the deep night. Dream me back and keep me by your side, by your side."

Harley had his eyes shut, voice soaring around the high notes, his hands still on the guitar while Joss's keys twined with the melody he drew out around him. Rose felt her body open up to the air around them, her soul expanding out of her back like wings and fusing with all the others swaying together and listening. Harley's lips brushed the mic as the music broke for Frank to join back in, building up to the guitar's return. He looked into the crowd, looked through the spotlights and the dark, and caught her eye.

She didn't think she'd be able to look away even if she wanted to. Her walls seemed to be cracked like a shell, exposing everything she'd always wanted to hide, all the vulnerability she hated so much, but it didn't seem to matter, didn't bother her at all for that one perfect moment. She stared back as he sang about one crystal moment, frozen and impossible to recapture, and she let her soul stand exposed until he dived back into the song again.

❖

"Did you hear, they've been asked to play the Solarium festival next year? They're headlining. Isn't that amazing?" Miho said as they drove back near midnight.

"Solarium? Isn't that the one down near Cheningwold?"

She nodded, tail lights reflected as red flickers in her glasses.

"I've been to that five years running," said Chelsea,

leaning forward with her hands on Rose's seat. "It's massive, and they always have freakishly good weather for mid-March. I can't believe they're really getting big. We'll be going to Wembley to watch them, just you wait."

Rose snorted. "We wouldn't get near the front there, would we?"

"Frank says we'll be in the wings, dancing like idiots," grinned Chelsea, keeping her voice down so Alicia didn't wake up.

Rose snickered. "We'd make too much noise."

"Yeah, I'd rather be down in the crowd anyway, telling everyone they're my friends."

"Think of the screaming girls," Rose said. "All the fans going mad as soon as they come onstage."

"Everyone wanting Harley to sign their boobs." Chelsea giggled.

Rose snorted so hard that Alicia blinked, then slumped back against the window and curled up again.

"Oh God, what an image." Miho scrunched her nose up. "I can see him being popular, though. He's so good looking."

Chelsea cocked her head. "You think? I dunno. Frank's got the muscles."

Rose raised her eyebrows. "If you think I'm going to be team Joss by default, you've got another think coming."

"Poor Joss." Chelsea sniggered. "She needs a makeover."

"And a hairstyle."

"And a hot meal. She'll have all the nanas after her."

"Oh my God, you're bad," Miho said, giggling into her hand.

"So if you're not team Harley or team Frank or, yeah, even team Joss," said Chelsea, shifting forward with the gleam of a gossip visible even in the dark. "Who would you get to sign your boobs?"

"*Chelsea.*"

Rose sighed. "Oh God, if he wasn't gay and attached, I'd be drooling over Max."

The car went silent. Even the radio seemed to get dead air. "What?" she said. "Oh, come on, like you wouldn't tap that if he was into girls."

"Max isn't gay," said Miho slowly.

"What? But...but he's with Jamie."

"No," Chelsea said with a nervous giggle. "Jamie's gay. But not Max."

"But they're always hanging off each other. And dancing together."

"You dance with me all the time. Does that mean we're dating?" said Miho, a little sharply. "Because I'd like dinner and a bunch of flowers, if so."

"They *live* together."

Chelsea bit her lip. "I mean, yeah, but that's not because they're together. They work together—"

"I don't live with my colleagues," she insisted because this was ridiculous. This was a total waste of time and energy for pining, and she was not ready to accept this. "And Jamie's really possessive over Max. Come on, you can't tell me that's platonic."

"Look, Rose, just..." Miho clenched her hands around the steering wheel and glanced at Chelsea. "I mean, it's not like it's a secret."

"What are you on about?"

Chelsea shrugged, and Miho glanced at her, one quick look before she had her eyes back on the road, but somehow, it was enough to pin her to her seat in silence. "Max is transgender," Miho said. "He lives with Jamie because his parents don't want him at home, okay? Jamie is his family."

Rose blinked. "Wait, but...really?" She frowned and

thought through every interaction she'd ever had with Max and Jamie. "He doesn't look like a girl."

Miho slapped her upside the head, and Chelsea leaned forward to do the same a beat after. "Ow! What the hell?"

"Do not even consider speaking to Max again until you've done some research, you hear?"

"Jesus, did you have to hit so—"

"Yes, we did," said Chelsea, leaning forward so far, she could almost glare at her eye to eye. "Max has been through a hell of a time. He deals with ignorant idiots every day, and he doesn't need any more from within our group."

"I'm not homophobic, oh my God."

"It's *transphobia* if it's about gender issues," said Miho, punctuating her words with thumps on the steering wheel. "See, this is why you need to get educated."

"Okay, look," said Chelsea, counting points off on her fingers. "You do not in any way refer to Max as a girl or even feminine. You do not ever consider him to be a girl who 'turned into' a boy. He's always been a boy, just assigned the wrong gender. You do not ask him whether he has a penis or not unless you want all of us to ask you whether you've got a fleshy labia—"

"Ew." Rose recoiled.

"Exactly. His pronouns are *he*, never anything else, especially not *it*."

"Okay, enough," she snapped, pushing Chelsea's hands down. "I'm not a complete idiot. And I'm not a bigot, all right? It took me by surprise, that's all."

The tension in the car hummed like a plucked string for a moment, then Miho nodded. "Yeah, okay. Sorry. Look, he's had a bad time. Chelsea and Jamie were at school with him, things are better now, but…"

"We look after our own," Chelsea said. "And that includes you, you know?"

Rose huffed a laugh. "One big happy family."

"Sometimes, you've got to make your own." Chelsea grinned and sat back.

CHAPTER SIX

With the Benefit of Hindsight

Rose did do some research. Honestly, she did. It was just that all the websites she found were so desperately worthy and irritating, and the vocabulary…Honestly, how many words did people need to define their exact position along the Kinsey scale, let alone the equivalent gender scale? But by the time she walked into Jericho to the next Stare at the Sun gig, she figured she'd learned enough to put it to one side. Max was a guy; that hadn't changed for her. He was still definitely her type, and even better, he wasn't actually gay. She didn't need to pretend she wasn't staring at him for Jamie's sake.

Harley saw her first as she walked into the hipster bar. "Hey, Rose. Can I get you a drink?"

"Yeah, thanks, that'd be good. I'm walking tonight."

"Bring on the alcohol," he said, and she snorted at his giddy silliness. "They do amazing cocktails here. Try the one with coffee."

"Oh God, I love coffee. I'll have that one, cheers."

Harley smiled like she'd praised his entire existence. Since Miho had told her about Harley's crush, she'd been watching him out of the corner of her eye. Sometimes, she thought Miho was deluded—she certainly seemed to think everyone else in the world was as in love with Harley as she was—but was she right about what he thought of other people? He certainly seemed to be watching her neck as she swallowed.

He bit his lip and turned away, and she cocked her head on one side. "Ready for the gig?" she asked before the lull became an uncomfortable silence.

"Yes," he said, back to his naive enthusiasm again. "This is one of the first places we used to play, even before Frank moved up here to join us."

"They'll have your photo framed and signed behind the bar before you know it," she teased.

"They do already, actually," he said, pointing at the big, green-framed mirror behind the bearded barman. "Or well, something like that. Lots of Polaroids, anyway."

"Well, look at that, famous already." She grinned and patted his shoulder.

It wasn't even a joke. Their fan base had shot up after Danny Howard had debuted "Easily Loved" on his Friday show. Since then, the other Radio One DJs had picked them up, and they'd gone from unpaid gigs in Oxford pubs and student unions to doing interviews for the "up and coming" pages of national music review magazines.

There was even talk of a second bigger tour. It was that point where they realised they might actually be on to a pretty big deal.

Harley opened his mouth, but Joss called him over, and he sighed. "I'll see you later, okay? After the gig?"

"Of course," she said, shrugging, and he smiled like she'd agreed to a freaking marriage proposal. Rose hopped onto the barstool and watched him across the thickening crowd. He looked back at one point and waved. She laughed, shook her head, and waved back.

She knocked back the last of her cocktail and bought

another, then wandered along toward the stage, trying to aim for Max. She could see him leaning over the amps to talk to Frank, his hips cocked, one knee bent up onto the dais, and *God*, he had such a nice arse.

"Rose! Hey, you got one of those coffee cocktails, huh? They're lush, aren't they?" Miho was practically jumping up and down in front of her.

"How many have you had?" She laughed.

"Oh, only three so far. I probably shouldn't have had so many. I think there's like three shots of espresso in here, maybe two, but either way, I don't cope very well with coffee. I'm a terrible stereotype, really. I get so hyperactive and twitchy and look, my hand's actually shaking, isn't that funny?" She laughed and held up her hand, which vibrated an inch in front of Rose's nose.

"Yeah, I'm appropriating that drink for your own good," Rose said. She glanced at Max, who was now standing back and tilting his head to listen to something Alicia was saying, her standing up on tiptoes to reach his ear. "Fine, come and get something to knock that caffeine high out. My treat," she said, hauling Miho back to the bar. "Honestly, the things I do for you."

"Ooh, can I have one of those sweet drinks with the banana and the Baileys? I love those. Or Tia Maria, maybe, mmm, that's delicious, don't you think? Or do you? What's your favourite spirit, Rose? Do you like Turkish delights, Rose, because they're rose flavoured, get it?"

"My God, you're wasted. No, I hate Turkish delights, and no, you can't have Tia Maria. That's coffee flavoured. No Coke, either, you really are a lightweight."

"I'm not. I drink loads of alcohol, you'll see. I'm not a lightweight at all. Ask Harley, I once drank six shots of

Sambuca in a row, and I didn't even throw up. Ask anyone. Or even better, I'll show you. Hey, Ron. Six shots of Sambuca, please?"

"No Sambuca," Rose said firmly to the barman, who just looked from one to the other with no expression whatsoever. "A pint of tap water, for a start."

"Is that all?" he asked, putting the lukewarm plastic cup in front of her.

"Can I at least have some cordial in it? Water's boring."

"Water's sensible. Drink up and I'll buy you that thing with the banana in it. Get something solid in your stomach to soak up the caffeine. Can you do a virgin version?" she asked the barman.

"Aw, no, don't do that. I can take the alcohol. It's the caffeine, caffeine has a funny effect on me. It makes me funny."

"It makes you ridiculous." She snorted. "Fine, on your own head be it. One of those banana cocktails, please."

"One Tropic of Capricorn, coming up."

"Tropic of...why the hell is it called that?"

He shrugged, and Rose wasn't convinced that he wasn't actually a robot. He was at least dead inside.

"Whatever." She shrugged. "Drink that water."

The band had started by the time they made their way back, Miho still chattering away at high speed beside Rose. Chelsea whooped and pointed when she saw them, also hyper. Rose hoped it was just regular drunkenness. She wasn't sure she could cope with two caffeine high idiots in one night. Especially when they were both quite squeaky girls to begin with.

Harley was bopping his crazy hair to "Summer Haze," and the crowd seemed to bounce up and down as one to the beat. Jamie was spinning front and centre with Alicia, then

Connor, then Aretha, and then Rose as she got too close, and he spun her around, too. By the time the drum outro finished in a clatter of cymbals, Rose was breathless with laughter, her head tipped back, her eyes unfocused with dizziness, and Jamie slung his arm over her shoulder and over some Italian guy on the other side of him, and they cheered.

Harley glanced over and caught her eye, his smile softening in some way she couldn't really understand. "This one's for you, Rose," he called, and she cocked her head, confused, as he started the soft, muted fingerings for "Across the Lines." She didn't know why he kept playing it, kept dedicating it to her. It had been a throwaway line, a tease because she knew it wasn't Tracy Chapman's most famous song. She didn't even know if it was her favourite. But they played it beautifully, heartbreakingly, and she closed her eyes to sway along to it.

She caught a glimpse of Max somewhere in the dreamy, sad song. He was swaying along, too, with someone else in the circle of his arms, and he was kissing her, a girl she didn't recognise, and wasn't that utterly typical?

It wasn't like she cared. She didn't care, why should she? She had no claim to him, she couldn't care less who he kissed, she already knew he wasn't gay, and well, it was just bad timing, wasn't it?

She swayed, though her jaw was clenching. She smiled and clapped for the band when they drew the song to a close, and she danced, she danced like a wild thing to the faster songs, threw herself into it because this was why she came. She had no interest in skinny white boys who clearly didn't consider her their type. Obviously, skinny white boys liked small white girls with big boobs, and she didn't care. Why the hell should she? She didn't care. She certainly didn't care when he was gone before the end of the gig, not like she was looking for him anymore. Stupid idea, anyway, thinking she should come and try to flirt with him tonight. Just because she now knew he wasn't gay didn't mean he'd ever be attracted to her.

"Can I kiss you?" Harley asked, his voice barely more than a whisper, and his head bowed close to her ear.

"What a good idea," she said, held his face still, and kissed him.

CHAPTER SEVEN

Girlfriend

"Oh God, what did I drink last night?" she groaned, clutching her head.

"Lots of everything, I think," said Harley, and she froze.

Oh yes. That had happened. That was a thing she'd done.

"Hey," she said. Or croaked. "Time is it?"

"Ten thirty," he said, then smiled and wrapped his arms around her, pulling her closer, snuggling into her neck. "Still early." He kissed her on the neck.

Rose stared up at the ceiling, hands linked over her stomach, wrapped up in him and a little too warm and embarrassed and somewhat…ashamed? She wasn't sure why. But he was comfortable enough. And her head really did hurt quite a lot. She closed her eyes and slipped back into sleep.

She woke up again around midday, and Harley was sitting up, cross-legged and holding out a cup of tea. "Morning, girlfriend."

Her brain stuttered. He didn't mean it like that, surely? What were they, twelve? Honestly, who did that, assumed they were girlfriend and boyfriend after one kiss? And, well, they'd done a bit more than that, but…

She shrugged and took the tea. "Oh, this is good tea."

His eyes lit up. "That's the way tea should be made. None of this stewing for hours business, just a quick dunk, and you're done."

She nodded and popped her neck. "And then you can use the same teabag for more than one cup. It's sensible."

"God, I can't believe you take your tea the same way I do. Everyone hates the way I make it. I mean, I hoped, but…"

"You hoped I'd take my tea the same as you?" She snorted.

"Well, no, that sounds…I just meant I hoped you wouldn't hate it, since I'd, like, made it for you, you know? But now it feels kinda perfect."

"Harley, it's just tea, mate."

His cheeks turned pink. "I know that."

She put the mug on the bedside table and slipped out of bed. Harley made a ridiculous squeaking noise and covered his eyes. Rose laughed. "You've seen me naked, Harley. You know, last night?"

"I know, but that was different. Anyway, I was trying to be respectful."

She laughed. "Very sweet but entirely unnecessary. I'm not self-conscious."

"Yeah, I'm getting that." He lowered his hands. She watched him in the mirror as she pulled her pants on and fastened her bra. His eyes flickered around the room as if he was going to get slapped for doing what she'd just given him permission to do, eventually watching her out of the corner of his eye as she pulled her jeans on and straightened her curls.

"Ah, do you want to do anything? Today?" he asked, clearing his throat.

"I've got to go food shopping. Boring stuff, but my fridge is empty."

"Oh, yeah. I used the last of the milk. Sorry."

"You brought me tea, don't be sorry." She shrugged.

"How about tonight?" he asked, looking up, hopeful.

She didn't answer as she cleaned the dregs of last night's

makeup off and pulled out her mascara to replenish it. Part of her wanted to say no, say it was a one-night thing, see you at the next gig. Part of her wanted to laugh at him, so eager and puppyish and in her cruelest thoughts, a little pathetic.

But she'd had fun last night. He was good in bed, that was for sure. He was good looking, and he was more of a gentleman than she'd ever been out with, if the tea was any indication.

And it wasn't like she had anything else going on.

"Yeah, okay." She shrugged.

❖

Harley left. Eventually. He went home to get changed, giving Rose a chance to do her Tesco run. He was, however, back before she was, dressed in a nice pair of jeans and a button-up shirt, standing outside her door with one leg hitched up against the wall, tapping his fingers awkwardly on his thigh. He jumped up as soon as he saw her coming up the street and took half the groceries.

"Hey," he said, slightly breathless.

"Hi," she said slowly. "You're early."

"Oh, yeah, I'm sorry. I hope that's okay? I, uh…" He laughed and rubbed the back of his neck. "I got keen. Sorry."

"Hey, don't be sorry." She shrugged. "I get someone to help me carry in my shopping. Win for me."

He smiled like he'd just won the lottery, and she turned her face away, making much more of a production of opening the door than it usually would be. She was still in her old trackie pants, she hadn't made any sort of effort with her makeup. She looked a mess, and Harley was dressed up for a date. Part of her cringed from the whole situation, embarrassed and ashamed, but the majority of her mind just didn't care. She felt like she was covered with a blanket of "what does it even matter?"

She took the bags from him, let him chatter as she put her shopping away, the thick layer of apathy numbing any guilt she had from leading him on or not trying hard enough for him.

"—get ready to head out in a bit."

"Huh?" she said, looking up.

Harley held his phone out. "The movie, it starts in an hour. Do you want to get something to eat first?"

Rose frowned and shook herself to clear the fog from her mind. "Sorry, yeah. If you like."

"What do you fancy? There's a nice restaurant—"

"Nah, the noodle shop's good," she said. And maybe there was a part of her that noticed him looking down as she walked into her bedroom to get changed, but if there was, it was quiet and suffocating under layers of cotton wool.

❖

The evening air seemed to blow some of the layers away, and she breathed deeply as they walked down the street. Harley linked his arm with hers, and she quirked a smile at him.

The car on the corner had the number plate FJW, and Rose snorted with memories of laughing so hard her ribs hurt. She nudged Harley and pointed at the car. "Hey, think of a phrase starting with those letters," she said.

Harley frowned in confusion.

"I mean, like FJW, let's see...French Jesus Wins." She grinned and turned to him. "Bit of a dumb one. Can you do better?"

He laughed and scrunched the hair at the back of his head. "Uh, I dunno, that one's pretty funny."

She frowned and pointed to the next car parked against the pavement. "Okay, try that one. RMP, oh my God, you've got to be able to think of something filthy for that one."

Harley scrunched up his face and shrugged. "I dunno, you're better at this than I am." He laughed. "Go on, what have you thought up for it?"

She looked at him, his face open and interested, and not... something.

"Nah," she said, turning back and walking toward the noodle place. She didn't look at the cars.

It wasn't so bad, she thought to herself. He was...nice. He was polite and good-looking and great in bed, and there was something addictive about being *wanted*. He bought her popcorn at the movies, he held her hand in the cinema, they went back to her flat and shagged again, and he curled around her with a smile on his face and fell asleep.

And she tried to tell herself that what she was doing was completely valid because, hey, it wasn't like she had anywhere else to be.

He left on Monday morning, kissing her for long minutes at her front door, and she tried not to look at her watch too pointedly because he was a sweet guy, and yeah, she'd always been a bitch, but was she going to have to actually kick him out just so she could leave?

She caught her bus. He texted her with kisses before she'd even arrived at the lab.

"Hey, Rose," said Andrea, her voice in that annoying lilt that everyone seemed to do when they had gossip, or they knew something they thought might be a secret, or they were about to tease you.

She raised her eyebrows. "Hi?"

"Anything you'd like to tell us?"

"Not particularly."

"Oh, holding out, huh? Not going to drop the latest gossip?"

"Andrea, there is no gossip. Do you not have a frog to squeeze or something?"

She shook her head. "Dave's harvesting the eggs today. Aw, come on, tell me about your new boyfriend."

She froze, then turned, straight-backed. "What?"

She held out her phone, Instagram open to a picture of Harley kissing Rose's cheek. "I knew you hung out with them but actually dating the lead singer? You took *Almost Famous* real seriously, girl."

Rose snatched the phone and read the caption. "'Finally convinced this girl to give me a chance, hashtag beautiful, hashtag bae, hashtag girlfriend'? Oh my God I just threw up in my mouth, Harley, what the fuck?"

Andrea snatched her phone back and clicked on Harley's profile. "You're such a cynic, I think it's romantic. I can't believe you guys are dating, you make such a cute couple."

Rose stared at her and fumed. "We're not…"

"Not what?"

She closed her eyes because she hadn't exactly said they weren't dating, had she? She'd let him call her girlfriend and let him take her out on a date, and she was now, apparently, *in a freaking relationship.*

"Nothing." She sighed.

"Tell me everything," Andrea squealed. "How long have you guys been dancing around each other? How did you get together? I want to know all the deets."

"Look, Andrea, I've got a lot to do, okay? Can you just… later, yeah?"

"Ugh, you're so boring, Rose. Fine. Lunch, though, you and me, we're going down to that café on the corner with the great lemon chicken baguettes, and you are going to spill."

She blinked, long and slow, and hoped that when she opened her eyes, Andrea would have burst into flames.

She was disappointed.

❖

Everyone knew by the time they got together for the next gig. Everyone seemed delighted for them, and Rose wondered what it was they'd all seen between her and Harley. Did they really give off some sort of "meant to be together" vibe? Everyone cheered and sat them together at any opportunity and cooed when Harley dedicated songs to her, and she tried to keep the frown off her face and see what they saw when she looked in the mirror.

There were times when she caught herself thinking she was doing the wrong thing, when a rush of panic flooded through her veins. Why was she the one sitting with her arm around Harley, rubbing his shoulder absently as he told her how nervous he was before getting onstage?

And then she'd look over at Max, sitting quietly by himself at the bar, giving her a nod as they caught each other's eye, and she turned away because this was better. Somehow. This was definitely better than something.

She danced as normal. She threw herself around with the Sunbirds. She laughed at Miho and banned her from drinking caffeine ever again. She sat with Connor and chatted to Alicia and Eliza and even Jamie and Max, and she kissed Harley whenever she felt like it and fell into bed with him, and it was all better than…than something. It was fine. It was becoming fun, she told herself. Harley bought her flowers and brought takeout over to her place, and told her she was beautiful, and she smiled, she really did.

Everything was fine.

Although maybe, when she started throwing up, maybe there was something that wasn't so fine after all.

CHAPTER EIGHT

Screw Up

"Oh God, no." Rose leaned against the sink, squeezing her eyes shut and fighting the panic rising in her throat. The two little lines were still there when she opened her eyes again.

"No. No, no, no, no. Shit." She sobbed the last word. The two little lines stared back at her like eyes, judgemental and perfect in their smug little white pen. She threw it across the room and hammered the heel of her hand on the side of the sink.

She took a deep breath and hung her head, then retrieved the pregnancy test and straightened her clothes. Time to sort this all out. The sooner the better. She threw the test in the kitchen bin so she wouldn't catch sight of it while she brushed her teeth, and then spent an extra-long time putting her makeup on.

"It'll be fine," she told herself firmly, scraping mascara viciously off the wand. "You'll book yourself into the family planning clinic, get an abortion, and pretend like it never happened."

She stopped and leaned her forehead against the glass. Sure. Because that was definitely how these things went. She felt the tears prickling at the corner of her eyes as she swore at herself, at condoms for not being a hundred percent effective, at contraceptive pills for giving her migraines. At the voice of her parents, wagging their fingers, saying "abstinence is the only way" in strong Timorese accents that two decades in Oxford hadn't squashed.

She gave up and let the tears flow. What would they think of her? How disappointed would they be? Mum would be secretly delighted. She'd always loved babies. She would've been an amazing grandma.

"It's irrelevant," she snapped out loud, glaring at herself in the mirror again. "They're not here to help, so they don't get to talk me out of it."

She glared at the tears pooling in her reflection's eyes until they disappeared. Then she sniffed, just once, and set about fixing her makeup.

CHAPTER NINE

Pregnant

The Solarium festival was held at a village a few miles southwest of Oxford. The band, and a lot of the Sunbirds, had decided to camp, for some unknown reason, in mid-March. They were just lucky it was freakishly warm. Driving in with the weight of new, unwanted knowledge, Rose was even more glad she'd resisted.

She pulled her access pass out to show the security guard and weaved through the sluggish crowds toward Frank's ridiculous van, but when she saw it across the field, her feet dragged to a stop, the stream of people jostling and flowing around her. Her hands clenched around the strap of her bag, and the mud squelched as she shifted her weight.

She'd walked straight to the pitch without thinking, like the day before. But it struck her that today wasn't like the day before at all. She was pregnant, and it was Harley's. Sure, it was a temporary thing, but it was a thing right now, and when she thought about it, it wasn't just her thing.

Harley probably had a right to know, she admitted, but if the decision had been made, did he really need to know? It was her body, after all. She was going to be the one dealing with the fallout. Especially the long-term fallout. Harley was lovely, but there was no way this was going to be forever. Honestly, she was amazed she'd let it go on this long. But she was always going to be the one carrying that mark in her mental calendar: *that was the year I had an abortion.*

Angry tears prickled her lower eyelids. Suddenly, she wanted him to know. It took both of them to make the foetus. He should have a share of the guilt for their irresponsibility. She could hear her dad saying, "The only guaranteed contraceptive is abstinence," like he had when she was a teenager. His newspaper had rustled as he lowered it to look at her dolled up for a night out. He'd even taken his reading glasses off to waggle them at her, emphasising each syllable. She'd rolled her eyes, even though she'd known he was right.

Someone moved across the van's window, and she jumped as the door slid open. Before she could see who came out, her twitchy muscles spun her around, and she walked toward the main stage with the current of people.

It took her a few seconds to justify running away to herself. She'd left because the sudden movement and sound had startled her, and adrenaline took over. But if the dopey-looking stranger walking beside her had turned to ask, she'd have told him she was protecting Harley and the rest of the band.

She couldn't tell him now. She couldn't even be near him in case the word *pregnant* was written across her head in blazing letters. This was the first time they'd ever been the headline for a proper festival, one with camping and overpriced stalls and an acoustic tent in the corner. Sure, it was Sunday in a small festival only in its third year. But it was still a big deal for them, and she didn't want to ruin anything about it.

Her phone buzzed in her pocket.

Hey gorgeous, what time u getting here?

For a moment, she considered lying, telling him she'd arrive just in time for them to go onstage at nine. But that was three hours away. What if they spotted her between now and then? That would screw with his head just as much.

Just browsing. Met up with some work colleagues, so I'll probs have dinner with them and shove my way down the front nice and early so I can see you front and centre.

Harley's reply came back immediately. *Nice. I'll come and meet you.*

Oh hell. She bit her lip and typed in a panic.

Oh no, you don't. The 3 of you stay together, what if you miss your cue?

Lol yeah that would suck. But I'm bored as the third wheel.

Ah, diddums. Don't worry, 3 hours will fly by.

It didn't.

Rose tried to distract herself from growing anxiety and boredom by browsing the hippy tat, merch stores, and stalls you could only ever find at a festival. There was one selling unusual musical instruments while a stoned-looking guy in a blue and yellow jester's hat, complete with bells, walked around with printed T-shirts for sale. Rose considered getting into the spirit a bit by buying a tie-dyed hoodie, but they didn't stock any that fitted her. Apparently, only skinny people were hippies.

She then queued up to buy a cheeseburger, her mouth watering in anticipation, but the moment she saw the grease dripping off the greyish meat, she had to race away from the van, stomach churning. It was as if the foetus, knowing her plans for it, was getting its revenge while it still could. She couldn't even seem to throw up, just walked around for the next hour dry heaving at every strong smell. She was tempted to stick her fingers down her throat and get it over with but ew. She still had standards.

Eventually, she found a grassy slope across from the main

stage and sat with elbows on knees to watch the crowd bob up and down to some arrogant ska band she'd never heard of. She hadn't even thought ska was a thing anymore, but there they were. The sun drifted below the low hills, and a shadow grew over her.

An emo band came back onstage for an encore, and after half-hearted cheers, Rose could hear the atmosphere in the crowd change. The pressure of people against her back increased as people shuffled close to the front, sealing the gaps so queue jumpers couldn't squeeze through. An excited ripple ran through in murmurs and shuffles whenever someone appeared onstage, mostly roadies setting up Harley's guitars in order and bringing out drums and keyboard stands.

Rose felt her own tummy getting butterflies and realised with a shock that her relationship was almost certainly going to come to an end when she told Harley about the pregnancy. She closed her eyes and tipped her head back to the star-speckled sky as the cocktail of frustration and guilt and regret overwhelmed her.

She didn't know what she'd do without the chaos and vitality of the Sunbirds. She'd never thought of music as being a particularly important part of her life, but the band had dragged her through some invisible barrier into a world of basslines and riffs, of people who knew your favourite song and dragged you out onto the dance floor. The thought of losing that now sent waves of panic through her gut. Even the old emptiness of life before the band was preferable to this uncertainty, and for a frantic moment she wished she'd never met them.

A cheer swept through the crowd as the band came onstage. Harley scanned the front few rows and smiled and waved when he spotted her. She grinned and shook her head. He was like a little kid going onstage at school, honestly.

"Hello, Glastonbury!"

The crowd giggled and whooped.

"Oh, sorry, that's next year, isn't it? Along with Wembley stadium and the world tour?"

"You've been forgetting to take your meds again, Harley?" Frank tapped out a *badum-tish* at his own joke.

"A boy can dream, right? But we fit in well here. Sunday at the Solarium festival, we are Stare at the Sun, and this is what we do."

They opened with a crashing two-four beat, marching their audience until heads whipped up and down and feet stamped. By the time they played their most upbeat song about dancing in an empty club, the whole crowd was leaping as one, shoulders pressed together to hold each other up. A mini mosh pit started behind Rose when they played their only political song, "Sins of the Fathers." She felt a sharp pang in her chest, remembering how he'd written that for her parents, all the family they'd left behind. And when they followed it with her favourite slow song, "Faust," she had to concentrate on square rooting random large numbers to stop herself from breaking down completely.

CHAPTER TEN

The Announcement

She took her time walking to the van, thinking about how his cute smile had grown on her over the past few months. Instead of just dancing and listening, she'd been watching him too, recently, how the hot lights caught on his loose curls and turned them to fire, drops of sweat carving a path to his neck as he sang. How his lips sometimes touched the mic like a kiss, and how he closed his eyes to hit the high notes. He'd always been attractive; that had never been in question.

This wasn't helping. She was supposed to be thinking about all his worst qualities so she wouldn't mind so much when the inevitable breakup came, but that was the thing. Harley was pretty low on actual faults, all things considered. He was the stereotypical nice guy, without the creepy privilege. Gentle, kind, thoughtful, he never reacted to her sarcasm. He was so laid back, he was horizontal.

It drove her crazy. And the fact that his equanimity infuriated her made her feel guilty. She knew he'd go along with whatever she decided to do with this pregnancy, let her make all the choices like he always did. He'd be right there with her, no matter what she wanted to do with a baby that was fifty percent his, and he'd probably be happy to stay together afterward, too. All the decisions would have to be hers. She'd have to choose the abortion. She'd break up with him because this…this was the tipping point.

For a moment, she felt bitter, that this was unfair, that she had to be the bad guy all the time. But wasn't that how she'd gotten into this? She was the bad guy. She knew he wanted her, and she wasn't that fussed about him, but she still fell into bed with him, fell into a relationship because why the hell not?

Well, this was a pretty good reason why not.

Harley was the only one in the van when Rose slid the door open. He was lounging on the double mattress Frank and Joss usually shared, fiddling with his acoustic twelve string. His eyes lit up when he saw her, and Rose felt a flare of anxiety and guilt, and then realised that she'd been feeling a minor version of that same flare for the past few months every time she saw how he felt.

"Hey, baby. Did you see us? What did you think?"

She half forced a smile. "You were awesome as usual. Where are the others?"

"They went to get some beers. Want me to text Frank to get you one?"

"No, I'm good. Want to go to your tent for a talk?"

He rubbed the back of his neck and grinned sheepishly. "I haven't put it up yet."

"Oh, Harley, it's dark now! When were you going to get round..." She stopped herself. "It doesn't matter. It really, really doesn't. Harley, I'm pregnant."

The colour drained from his face, and his eyes widened. "You're what?"

Rose clenched her jaw. His reaction was completely as expected and all the more annoying for it. "Pregnant. Gravid. A foetus has implanted its little parasite self into the lining of my uterus, and since it's fifty percent your fault, you can drive me to the abortion clinic as soon as I find the nearest one and get an appointment. Or the hospital. Wherever these things happen outside movies."

She shut her mouth with a click, crossing her arms, irritated with herself for losing her composure and being so bitchy. Harley's eyes were wide, and his mouth was hanging open as he stumbled to his feet, tripping over the neck of his guitar. "No. You can't be—"

"I am, though. Did the test and everything."

"No, no, no. Please…I mean don't have an abortion. Please, Rose, you can't get rid of it."

Rose stared at him and laughed once, a sharp sound. "Are you kidding me? You're in a rock band, you can't possibly be a…a pro-lifer or whatever."

"I'm not, I just…" He grabbed her arms and knelt in front of her, rocking the van. With her still standing outside, they were the same height now. "Please, Rose, not my baby."

She shoved his hands off her arms and stepped back, staring. "But it's my body."

"I know, and I'm really sorry. If I could carry it, I would, but I'll never be able to do that, and I might never get another chance."

She laughed, a cruel edge sneaking in. "I'm sure if you screw enough people, you'll manage it again."

"No, you don't understand."

"No, *you* don't understand, Harley. I'm not having a baby. I've never wanted kids. I'm not mother material. I don't want to leave my job."

"You won't have to. I'll quit the band. I'll look after the baby."

"You'll what? Don't be a bloody idiot. You've just been signed. This is what you always wanted."

"I want this more, Rose, please, please don't do this. I'll do anything."

"Hey, Rose." Joss's yell distracted Harley, whose feet were still tangled in Frank's duvet, and Rose took her chance to turn sharply and walk through the other campervans quickly, hiding from their view.

She couldn't get his face out of her head, the sharp, fearful clarity of his eyes, teeth almost bared as he begged her. Harley had never even had an opinion on anything, and while he was passionate about music, his friends, her, she'd always felt like he didn't really have an aim. He played music because he loved it. Whether other people wanted to listen was incidental. He treated Rose with a sort of reverence that made her feel uncomfortable and unworthy, and she couldn't deny his passion in bed, but he didn't fight for things. So this sudden ferocity was scary.

The main stage was dark, the crowd dispersed to bed or one of the beer or DJ tents. Rose sat, shivering on a bench, her hands fisted deep inside her pockets.

Her phone rang, but she heard his voice before she pulled it out. "There you are."

The ringtone cut out as Harley pressed the screen of his own mobile and held his hands out toward her as if she had a gun. "I'm calm now. I'm sorry, please don't go."

When she didn't run again, he walked forward slowly and sat next to her. "Thank you. I'm sorry if I scared you before."

She relaxed her tense muscles one by one. "That's not it. You blindsided me, that's all." She hunched herself up into her coat collar. "This wasn't how I expected it to go."

"You're telling me." He snorted. "I'm supposed to be infertile."

"You what?" She sat up and turned to stare, gaping.

"Mumps when I was fifteen. How old-fashioned is that? It was a really bad strain. I was off school for almost a month. The joys of anti-vax parents, huh? Anyway, the doctors said my sperm count was next to nothing."

"You always use condoms."

"Yes, Rose." He rolled his eyes, and that was a shock in itself. "STDs. You may have heard of them, being a biologist."

"What I meant, you ass, is how the hell did this even happen? What are the chances?"

"Practically zero. It's a miracle, Rose." He grabbed her hand, pulling it out of her pocket, the feverish look back in his eyes. "Which is why I'll do anything. Please, I've always wanted children, and this is probably my only chance."

"I didn't know you wanted kids," she said softly rather than pulling her hand away.

He shrugged. "I've wanted kids since I was a kid. I always stole my sister's dolls when my dad wasn't looking. But it's not a very manly thing, is it? It's acceptable for a girl to want kids, but everyone always assumes if a boy wants kids that he must be gay. Ironic, huh? And then after the mumps, there didn't seem to be any point in bringing it up."

His eyes had drifted over to the field of tents as he spoke, but he snapped his attention back to her again, all sharp and intense and completely unlike himself. "I will pay you, Rose. Name your price and I'll make sure you get it."

She pushed him off, curling her lip, and he grabbed her again. "No, don't look all disgusted. You don't want this baby, and I do, and I physically can't have any others. I'm not prepared to find a more willing girl and rely on lightning striking twice. You don't even have to stick around afterward, think of it as surrogacy."

He gazed at her in the night, the distant sounds of parties echoing around them, somewhere outside this bubble of unreality they were trapped in. "Don't decide now, okay? Just think about it for a couple of days. Look, meet me for lunch on Tuesday at that Pret down the road from you, and tell me then. Is noon okay?"

She nodded, mute, and he took her phone out to write a reminder in her calendar. "Jesus, Harley, are you a pod person or something?"

He grinned, his eyes still fever bright, and left her.

CHAPTER ELEVEN

Contract

It was ridiculous. Rose curled around a hot water bottle and stared into the grey morning light filtering through the curtains. Utterly ridiculous. She was going to go into that meeting and tell him she definitely still wanted an abortion. After all, she'd been up since four in the morning hurling her guts up. No way was she going to do this for nine whole months.

She dragged herself out of bed and stared at herself in the mirror. Her hair was greasy and heavy, her breasts were sensitive, and her stomach felt hollow and empty. "It's the morning sickness," she told herself. "That's all."

She turned away, her eyes skittering over the picture of her parents. "I'm not ashamed," she told the fridge as she got milk out for tea. "I have nothing to be ashamed about."

"I mean," she said as she poured the hot water over her tea bag. "It must be a misdiagnosis. He's not as infertile as everyone thought."

That must be it. It wasn't Harley's last chance. He was fine. He'd fall in love with a nice girl, someone who wasn't using him as a distraction. She swallowed hard as the shame swelled up again and pushed it back. She was not ashamed. He would fall in love with someone nice, she would love him back, and they'd get married and have nice babies.

She wondered again what her parents would say. What would they think about Harley? Would they wish she was a little bit nicer? Would they wish she actually loved him? What would be worse, in their eyes? That she was pregnant out of wedlock, or that she was refusing to help someone?

❖

Harley looked almost as nervous as she felt when she walked into the Pret A Manger two days later. Seeing him bite his cuticles and jog his knees, foot resting on the neighbouring chair, gave Rose the strength to force her own anxiety down as she walked toward him. All business, she told herself. Forget you've seen him naked…gloriously naked.

She banished the image from her mind firmly, and sat.

"Rose." His face lit up, dimples appearing around the edge of his grin, and she dredged up an answering smile.

"Harley." Her voice was as businesslike as she'd been hoping, but the guilt jabbed at her when his smile faded. *Put the poor guy out of his misery, for God's sake.* "All right. I'll be your surrogate. But that's all this is."

She held up one finger, cutting off the gasp of thanks, the excitement visibly bubbling under his skin. If she let him, he'd be grabbing her off her chair and kissing her right now. "Listen, Harley. I don't want a baby. I don't want children. I never have, and I never will. I'm happy to be able to give you what you want, but please don't think this is one of those shitty rom-coms where the kid brings two people together in the end. I'll have your baby, but that's it for us. We're not raising it together. We can't stay together."

The smile was completely gone now, and he was picking at his cuticles again. After a moment, just enough time for Rose to swallow the inexplicable lump in her throat, he looked up at her and nodded.

Those damn puppy eyes nearly made her change her mind.

She could probably train herself to be somewhat nurturing, couldn't she? For him?

But that was the problem, she realised, her resolve crystalising. She didn't want him, not in the long run. He was gorgeous and funny, kind and fantastic in bed, but she didn't love him. She felt her cheeks darken with shame when she admitted to herself that he'd always wanted her more than she'd wanted him. Maybe if she'd loved him, they could have made this work. And maybe it would have torn them apart anyway. She stood and turned to go, not looking at him.

"Rose, wait, please. I...I want to be around for the pregnancy as well, at least some parts. Please?"

She suppressed a groan and wondered if she could pretend that wasn't a perfectly reasonable request. "Okay, what sort of things?"

"Well, for a start, when's the due date?"

Rose's face burned again. "I actually have no idea. Like, nine months' time, I guess?"

He laughed, and she glared at him. "No, sorry, sorry," he said, waving his hands at her. "I'm not laughing *at* you, I just...look, there's a calculator online. I found it."

He pulled out his phone and started tapping away at his internet bookmarks. She lowered herself back down, tucking her handbag under her chair. This was probably something she should put into her diary, after all.

"Okay, here we go. When did your last menstrual period start?"

She frowned but pulled up her period tracker app. "January seventh."

"Great, I'll put that in. Here we go. The baby's due on the fourteenth of October. You're nine weeks along." He smiled down at his phone. "Wow. An autumn baby." He shook himself slightly. "Uh, what else...when's your first ultrasound?"

She shrugged helplessly. "I didn't even know this was a thing until two days ago, Harley."

"Well, have you called your doctor? You could do it now, if you like, I'll wait." He looked at his phone again. "I mean, they don't do the first ultrasound until twelve weeks, so there's still plenty of time." He looked up and blushed. "Sorry, I'm going to be completely obsessed and read those websites that compare his or her size to a piece of fruit each week."

"Oh, Harley." She sighed. "I wish this could be different. I'm sorry I'm not—"

"Hey, don't worry about it." He smiled, but it was a shallow copy of the usual blinding grin. "Sorry, I've always been broody. Guess I'm just a big girl."

"Nothing wrong with being a girl, big or otherwise."

"Yeah, tell that to my dad." He snorted.

Rose resisted the urge to take his hand and gathered her stuff again. "My lunch break's nearly over. I'll text you when I get an ultrasound date, if you want to come. No, scrap that, you have to come. This is your baby, not mine."

He stood with her. "Thank you. Are you coming to the gig in Coventry on Thursday?"

She blinked. "You really think that's a good idea?"

"Of course. We're still friends, aren't we?"

Her heart sank at the wide, fake smile. "Harley, I'm—"

"Besides, I've read that babies can hear from inside the womb. I want him or her to be introduced to the best music there is." He spread his arms wide, and she couldn't help but laugh.

"Fine then, maestro. I'll see you there."

CHAPTER TWELVE

Splinters

"What's this I hear about you breaking my best mate's heart?"

Rose turned to face Frankie as he dropped his bulk into an armchair at her table. The pub was quiet, still, and most of the others were at the bar. Rose couldn't tell how serious Frankie was or how much he knew.

Before she could reply, he laughed. "You look like a rabbit in the headlights, girl. Relax, it's none of my business."

She sighed in relief and went back to texting Andrea.

"But you have broken up, right?"

She raised an eyebrow. "What happened to 'none of my business'?"

He shrugged. "I'm nosy, and Harley's lovesick sighs are gusting so hard, my high hats are constantly vibrating."

She winced. "He said he still wanted us to be friends."

"Yeah, that always works out." He snorted. "Harley's been crazy about you since he first met you. You breaking up with him isn't going to change that."

"You and Harley broke up?" Miho's voice pitched even higher than usual, and Rose groaned to see her and half the Sunbirds settling into seats around them.

"Thanks a lot, Frankie," she grumbled.

"I think that's my cue to sound check," he replied and winked as he left her surrounded by all the others.

"What happened?" asked Miho. The girl looked like she was about to cry, like Rose had just broken up with *her*.

"It didn't work out," Rose said awkwardly. Harley had asked her not to tell anyone about the baby until the twelve-week mark, some sort of superstitious nonsense. But whatever, it was his baby.

"But he's crazy about you." Miho was almost flapping, and the rest of the group was watching like they needed popcorn.

"Yeah, Miho, but it takes two to tango, and I didn't want to dance anymore."

"Is this some kind of joke to you?" Miho stood, thin white fists clenched so Rose could see the blue veins standing out.

"Why are you so upset about this? You're acting like this is a personal insult."

"I don't know how you can do this to him." She crossed her arms and stuck her chin out. "You knew how he felt about you before you got together. How could you put yourself in a position where you knew you were going to break his heart?"

Rose jumped to her feet, towering above her. "For God's sake, Miho, you should be happy about this. He's all sad and pathetic now, perfect for you to finally act on that crush you've been nursing forever."

She regretted it as soon as she said it. She expected Miho to turn and walk away when the blood drained from her face, and she was scrambling to find a way to take the cruel words back. But Miho stepped closer to her and spoke quietly. "That's the difference between you and Harley. He knows he can't love me the way I love him, so he doesn't take advantage."

She turned on her heel and marched out, followed in a scramble by Alicia and Chelsea. Connor stood as well and shook his head at Rose. "She's right, you know."

Rose did know. She'd known since she woke up next to Harley for the first time, since the first time she'd seen him smile in his sleep and tangle his limbs with hers, since every time he'd looked at her as if she was made of magic. She kept her eyes firmly to the floor as she escaped to the toilets to hide her tears.

❖

"Rose? You all right in there?"

Rose jumped as Max shoved the door to the ladies' open, his hand over his face like something about the bathroom was going to blind him. She laughed and sniffled into her tissue. "It's fine. It's empty. You can come in if you like."

"Yeah, no." He snorted.

"Fine." She sighed. "Give me a min to do my makeup." He closed the door again. She finished her mascara and eyeliner, then took a deep breath and glared at the mirror before walking out. Max was leaning against the wall, his long-sleeved T-shirt rolled up to his elbows, one heel kicked up to rest on the wall behind him, proper James Dean style. She wasn't too depressed to enjoy the picture.

He raised an eyebrow, and she huffed, leaning back against the wall next to him. "You okay?" he asked.

"Sure. I guess I deserved that."

He shook his head. "I don't think so. Miho's letting her emotions get in the way. It's really none of her business."

"I should have stayed away, though. I knew he liked me way more than I liked him."

"There's always going to be a bit of that," Max said, fiddling with his lip piercing. "You can't avoid a relationship because you don't love someone going into it. Sometimes love grows. You could have fallen for him a few months or years after getting together, but you didn't, and that's your business. You did what's right for you, right?"

Rose nodded, but her lower lip was starting to do some humiliating wobble. She bit it hard, but he noticed, looped an arm around her, and kissed her hair. She gulped, partly shock, partly relief, and the tears fell again.

"Sorry," she said. "Damn it. Got to do the makeup again."

"Go on," he said with a half-smile. "I'll wait again."

She smiled up at him and went to repair her face for the third time.

❖

She tried to lose herself in the music and the dancing again, but everything had been jolted sideways, and it was all her fault. There was a clear division between people who agreed with Miho, and those who stood by Rose or just didn't care enough. It was no surprise that Alicia and Chelsea were on Miho's side; the trio was joined at the hip already. Connor had been a bit of a surprise, and Rose looked away from them when the squaddie met her eyes with a venomous glare.

At least Max was on her side, she thought, then felt selfish and guilty. She shouldn't be here, splitting up this group of friends. They'd been Harley's for ages before she'd even met them, and she didn't deserve to have any of them. But she couldn't help the grateful feeling when Jamie, Aretha, and Eliza all spoke to her like nothing had changed.

"Sorry about my brother's big mouth," Eliza said in her ear between songs.

"It's fine. People would have found out soon enough."

Eliza shrugged and left it at that, throwing herself into another wild dance. As Rose followed, twisting her hips less than usual, she wondered how much it would change again when the pregnancy was announced.

CHAPTER THIRTEEN

Ultrasound

"Lie back and roll your T-shirt up. Can I tuck this paper towel in the waistband of your jeans?"

Rose popped the button on her jeans and shoved them low on her pelvic bone. There was definitely going to have to be some shopping in the future, but until she couldn't bear the pressure of her current trousers, there was no way she was going to spend money. Clothes shopping sucked enough when she actually wanted the damn things.

The technician squirted warm gel on her tummy and pressed down hard with the scanner. Rose winced and clenched her pelvic floor muscles, wondering how many women wet themselves at these things.

The technician smiled at her as if sensing her discomfort. "You don't have to come with a full bladder to the next one. The uterus will be bigger and closer to the surface by then. Ah, here we are." She pointed to a moving alien shape on the screen. Rose narrowed her eyes and was about to make a sarcastic observation when Harley grabbed her hand. His eyes were filled with tears.

Rose clicked her mouth shut and turned away, back to the little squirming thing on the screen. It took the technician a while to get a still photo, to take the measurements for the Down's syndrome test, and Harley chatted to her belly, a huge smile on his face. He encouraged it to stay still for the nice lady, joked that it was going to be a handful, and all the while, Rose could feel herself getting more and more distant from the whole situation. It was like she was standing outside a glass box in the dark, watching Harley and the technician bond with the interloper in her inanimate body.

"Do you want a photo?"

Rose blinked, snapping back to herself. Harley was nodding like a toddler offered cake. "Yes, please. Rose, do you want a copy?"

"Nah." She stretched and wiped the gel off her still flatish tummy. "I've got the thing right here. I don't need to see it." She fake-grinned at the surprised technician. "Mind if I go to the loo now?"

Harley was standing in the foyer waiting when she came out of the ladies'. He was cradling the photo in both hands, making doe eyes at the blurry black-and-white bean in the middle. Rose couldn't help smiling when he beamed up at her. He pulled her into a half hug and kissed her temple. This is fine, she thought. Friends do this.

But friends didn't usually carry each other's children.

"You're coming to the gig in Cowley tonight, yeah? I'd like to tell everyone, then, if you're okay with that?"

"Sure," she said, with a nervous whoosh of air. Well, things with Miho couldn't get much worse, could they?

❖

She stood in front of the full-length mirror on the inside of her wardrobe door. There still wasn't any sign of anything under her skin. She lifted her shirt, slipped her jeans off, and stared hard at her belly. It was the same as always. Not really flat, it never had been, but the layer of chub around her waist was the same as ever. What would it look like in a few weeks? A few months? She pushed her tummy out, leaned back with her hand on her lower back. It just looked like she had a backache.

She snorted, changed her jeans for a sparkly pair, and pinned her long hair up with a couple of carved wooden sticks. She was already late to meet everyone before the gig. This was all procrastination. At least she only had to cross the road to get to the O2. Same place she'd first met them all almost a year ago.

The queue was a whole lot bigger this time, even an hour before the show, so she slipped down an alley to the back door and texted Eliza to let her in. She heard them before the door opened, a herd of elephants thundering down the narrow, unpainted staircase before Eliza threw it wide, phone in hand.

"Congratulations," they all yelled together, whooping, eyes wide and smiles wider.

Rose scrunched her face up in a pathetic imitation of a smile. "He told you. Yay."

They grabbed her and pulled her in, hugging her and passing her along to the next, dragging her upstairs and into the green room. "Does this mean you guys are getting back together?" yelled Chelsea.

"No," snapped Rose. "Harley, can I talk to you, please?"

He looked up from his conversation with Frankie and did a bit of a deer in the headlights impression. Good, she thought, as she grabbed his wrist and pulled him out of the green room and into the stairwell. She could hear Max singing "awkward," dragging out the last syllable, as the door shut behind them.

"What's up, Rose? I thought you were okay with me telling them."

"But *what* did you tell them? About us, I mean. Why do they think we're getting back together?"

"I didn't. I told them about the baby, I didn't say anything else."

"So they assumed we'd be getting back together to have the baby. Is that what you wanted them to think? Are you trying to manipulate me back into a relationship with you or something?"

"What? No. Of course not, I—"

"You what?"

He turned to the side slightly, rubbing his fingertips through the thick hair at the back of his neck. "I wanted to keep your options open, you know? A lot of things change when kids come along. You say you don't want kids right now, but when you feel the baby move, when he or she is actually here, you'll change your mind. You might even love me like I—"

"Oh God, Harley, don't say it."

"I love you, Rose."

"Oh…oh shit." She clamped her hands over her nose and mouth, then covered both eyes. "Harley, Jesus, no. I'm not going to fall in love with you. And you can't expect the baby to make me. That's not fair on any of us. I never felt anything like that for you, and I'm so sorry. I sort of knew you felt much more for me than I ever did for you, and I probably should have ended it when I realised there was no future for us, but I'm selfish, and I thought, you know, we're young, nobody's looking for a future at this age, and oh God."

She ran out of breath and looked at him between her fingers. He was still standing facing slightly away from her, chewing his lip and staring at the floor. He took a deep breath and looked straight at her, his eyes hard. "In that case, I want you to sign something. Some legally binding thing to say you give up your claim to custody, that you're just a surrogate."

"Harley, you already know—"

"No, I don't know. I don't *know* anything, and neither do you. There are all these stories of surrogates changing their mind, realising they want to be a mother after all, and I don't…I cannot trust that you're not going to do that to me halfway through."

Rose stared, in awe of this ferocity. He turned back to the wall, fists clenched and teeth working at his lip again. She nodded. "Okay, I'll sign it. If it makes you feel better. But I'm not going to change my mind."

His face softened, and his shoulders relaxed, and he turned to give her a tiny smile. "Thanks. I won't bar you from ever seeing him or her. And if you do change your mind because things like that do happen, yes, even to you…well, we can put in a clause about joint custody. But I want to be the main caregiver. I've fought for this baby's life already, Rose. Don't think I won't do it again."

"Sure thing, Mama Bear," she said, thumping him gently on the shoulder. "Let's go explain it all to the others. Nosy bastards that they are."

Harley smiled back, his old dimpled grin, and put his hand on her back to escort her through the door. "Can't do anything the easy way, can we?"

"That would be boring."

Chapter Fourteen

Not the Easy Way at All

They explained the situation together. It was met with stunned silence, and was, as Max muttered to Jamie, no less awkward. Miho opened and closed her mouth a few times before stomping out. Alicia and Chelsea gave Rose the stink-eye before following, and she wondered in amusement if they actually cared about the situation or if they were just blindly loyal to Miho.

Eliza broke the silence. "So what are you going to do about the tour next year, Harley?"

"Huh?"

"Don't you dare look at me like that, you brainless idiot, I am this far from a nervous breakdown about it already. What are you going to do with a tiny baby while you're on tour?"

"I haven't actually…"

"Of course you haven't."

He turned to Rose slowly. "I don't suppose…"

"No, Harley, I'm your surrogate, not the kid's mother."

"Well, you kind of are," muttered Frank.

"Screw you, Francis," she snapped. "Why do you think I wanted an abortion?"

"Slut," he hissed.

"Hey, that's enough," Max said, he and Jamie both stepping forward. Joss looked horrified and slapped her boyfriend. Max put his hand on Rose's shoulder. Frankie just snorted into his beer and shook his head.

"Yeah." Rose looked at Harley. "I think I'll be off."

"No, Rose, please."

"I'll play your EP every night, I promise. But you can all get fucked if you think I'm sticking around for this."

She turned around and stomped back downstairs, making as much noise as possible, as if she could expel all her fury by stamping like a toddler. Hot tears were tracing their way down her cheeks as she burst out into the alley, pulling her cardi across her chest when the light drizzle hit.

She was almost at the crossing when a heavy hand fell on her shoulder. She reacted instantly, spinning to catch the hand with a rolling grasp and striking at the face with the heel of her other hand.

"Whoa, whoa, whoa, God's sake, karate kid. Jesus, take it easy."

Rose controlled the strike inches before it smashed Jamie's nose and stepped back.

"What the hell was that, Rose?"

She shrugged. "Karate."

"That was badass," crowed Max, catching up and leaning on Jamie's shoulder, wheezing.

"Mate, you need to quit smoking." Jamie laughed. Max shrugged and lit a cigarette, pressing at the centre of his chest.

"What are you guys doing here?" she demanded, shaking the adrenaline out of her arms.

"Getting beaten up by the looks of it. You a black belt or something?"

"Blue. Got my brown belt grading in a few weeks." She huffed. "Guess that'll have to be put on hold now."

"Nah," said Jamie, flapping his hand. "My sister was

mucking out and riding every day until the morning before she popped. Just take it a bit steadier."

"You guys have horses?" She grinned. "Always knew you were a bit posh."

"We're farmers, love. Would you call the Wurzels posh?"

"To be fair, you are actually a bit of a gentleman farmer, Jamie," Max added.

"Does that make you my serf or vassal or something?"

Max grinned, a deep dimple appearing on his left cheek, and dropped his cigarette butt in a drain, blowing the last lungful of smoke away from Rose. "Are we going to stand here all night, or have you got a destination in mind?"

"You guys should go back to the gig. It's nice of you to come after me, but I don't want to lose Harley any friends."

"We're not playing favourites here," Max said, shaking his head. "We'll go to all the other gigs, maybe, but what Frank said was not okay. Joss was furious with him when we left."

"But you guys have been friends with them for ages. You barely know me."

"I know when my friends are wrong," muttered Max.

Jamie patted him on the back cheerfully. "So where to?"

"I was just going to go home." She sighed, rubbing her forehead. "You're welcome to come over if it's not too boring."

"Netflix and chill?" Max grinned, eyebrows waggling. Rose smacked his arm and led them up the road to her little flat.

They drank tea and spread themselves on the bean bags and two-seater sofa in her sitting room, talking and laughing. It was two in the morning before Rose finally checked the time on her microwave as she prepared the fifth round of tea. Jamie had fallen asleep, curled into a nest of bean bags, and Max was yawning when he took the cup she held out. She skritched his scalp, and he moaned into his drink. "I've seduced people for less," he warned.

She laughed and stomped on something under her ribs. Maybe she was starting to feel the foetus move or something. This was fine. This was good. Friends were, she'd been told, a good thing to have, and they were a little thin on the ground.

She slipped down onto the sofa, and Max leaned against her shoulder, eyes falling shut. Rose finished her tea and rescued Max's cup as he slid down to rest his head on her lap in his sleep. She brushed her fingers through his inky black hair, silky strands slipping across her skin and falling on his pale cheek. His long legs dangled off the side of the sofa.

Friends were a good thing.

Chapter Fifteen

Hush

Rose woke up to the smell of bacon and eggs, and two guys in rumpled button-downs making coffee and toast. "Oh my God," she moaned when they put a plate and a mug in front of her. "I freaking love you guys."

The tears came as a surprise. She couldn't seem to stop them, possibly because they'd caught her unawares, and she was soon gulping and ugly crying into Max's shoulder while Jamie stroked her back.

"Pregnancy hormones, huh?" Max grinned once she'd gotten herself under control.

"No." She hiccupped. "I just really feel that strongly about bacon."

They laughed and got their own breakfast before joining her once more. "What're you boys up to today?" she asked, wiping brown sauce off her chin.

"Bit of drilling down at West Field," Jamie replied, more to Max than her. "And Starkey's Way needs spraying."

Max nodded. "Late night, then."

"Or early morning, depends when the wind picks up. Combine needs servicing, too."

Rose nodded sagely. "I have no idea what you two just said."

"Come on." Jamie laughed. "Everyone knows what a

combine is. You must've heard the 'Combine Harvester' song. No? You're a proper townie, you are."

"And you sound more and more like a farmer when you talk about it."

Max was fiddling with his phone, mouth full of food, and Rose jumped when a brass instrument blared from the little speakers.

"Blimey," Jamie laughed. "You've got the Wurzels on your phone?"

"You haven't?" Max grinned. The two of them sang along with some of the most ridiculous lyrics Rose had ever heard and cackled over the rest of them. She laughed too as the song came to an end.

"What even is that?"

"Oi, that's a Young Farmers staple, that is."

"Young Farmers?"

"We'll take you to the next ball or AGM. You think uni students are bad on a night out? Young Farmers are next level ridiculous."

She shook her head. "That is…incongruous."

"Give us time." Jamie grinned. "We'll teach you the way of the Young Farmer." He checked his watch and slapped Max's knee. "C'mon, string bean. The countryside awaits."

Rose stood to hug them both good-bye. "Thanks, guys. I really appreciate you sticking around last night."

"No worries." Max smiled as he squeezed her arm, his dimple showing again. "You've got my number, yeah? Give me a call if you need anything. I'll be busy with harvest soon, but I can talk while I'm driving up and down a field."

"Only if you get a hands-free kit for the John Deere," Jamie yelled as he tugged his coat on.

Max groaned. "Do I have to drive that piece of junk?"

Jamie smacked the back of his head and leaned in to kiss

Rose's cheek. "Do call us if you need anything. Chat, foot rub, booty call. Well, maybe Max more than me for the last one, but whatever."

Max punched his arm, and Rose laughed as they bickered on the way down the stairs.

It was oppressively quiet when she closed the door, and she turned some shitty weekend TV programme on to fill the vacuum while she lay on the sofa. Last night had been precious, but it wasn't going to be much of a replacement for the social life she'd lost. Stare at the Sun gigs had been her only entertainment for almost a year now. Was she going to fall back into working overtime, watching mindless TV, and falling into bed at nine to wake up exhausted and late for work? Without the band and the Sunbirds, she hardly ever went out. Andrea and the others in the labs had long given up on her, and though Jamie and Max were being lovely, it was just the wrong time of year for them.

Her phone chimed, and she wriggled until she could get it out of her pocket. Harley.

Sorry about Frank. U OK?

Rose scrunched her face up and considered her reply. *Yeah, I'm fine. Not your fault. Gig OK?*

Yeah, good turnout. Don't suppose I can convince you to come to the next one?

Sorry, Harley, too soon. I really will play your CD to the baby tho.

There was no reply for a few minutes. Rose smacked herself in the face and wrote again. *You're still welcome to see the bump as it grows, just not at gigs.*

It was another minute or two before the reply came through. *Ever heard of NCT?*

No.

Harley sent her a web link. *I want to go. It'll be a lot less*

*awkward if you're there, too, and we might learn something.
I'll pay, obvs.*

Rose took a moment to read the site, horror growing by
the minute. *Just what I've always wanted, the chance to be
judged by a group of middle-class white people.*

Aw, it won't be that bad.

Why do you want this again?

*All the message boards I've been on say it's a great way
to meet other parents and get a support network. My family's
all in the States, Frank and Eliza are being weird about it, and
I know I won't have you anymore.*

Rose let her phone fall onto her face and wallowed in guilt
for a moment before she remembered she was growing another
human in her own flesh for him. *You owe me, Stevenson.*

Thank you. You won't regret this.

"Ugh," she muttered to herself. "I think I already do."

Not nearly as much as she regretted ever hearing of a
thing called Facebook, though. She opened the app on her
phone and almost threw it to the other side of the room in fury
and disgust.

The whole situation, the battle lines and commentary
and speculation, was laid out for everyone to see. People
were congratulating her and Harley, congratulating Harley
by himself, exclaiming at the exciting news, and a ridiculous
number of women informed her that this was going to be the
most exciting stage of her life, as if they'd all become psychic
because they'd once pushed a squirming, squalling creature
out from their vaginas.

Harley, all credit to him, hadn't started it. That had been
a drunken Connor congratulating him on his impending
fatherhood, and it had gone viral within their growing fanbase.
Harley had posted a scan of the ultrasound and made it very

clear that Rose had kindly agreed to be his surrogate and make his dreams come true. Sodding HuffPost had picked up the story and written an editorial on masculinity in parenthood and how important it was to have representation in "the black community" and the music industry. They then speculated that he was gay, therefore undermining their whole damn article, and Rose left a comment saying as much.

As she pressed send, she saw things from Harley's point of view a little clearer. She clicked back on Facebook.

You'll be an epic dad, Harley. It's my privilege to make that possible for you.

Then she deleted her account. She barely used it anyway.

She was in work early the next day, but there were still excited people there before her, patting the chub on her tummy that hadn't actually grown yet and telling her she was already showing, asking to see the ultrasound, asking if she was going to co-parent with Harley.

"No," she said through gritted teeth. "I'm just the surrogate."

"Oh," said a flustered Andrea, and Rose felt slightly guilty. It wasn't her fault two other people had already asked the same question. "But I thought you and Harley were together."

"We were." She sighed and relented. "But I've never wanted kids, and he desperately does." Andrea looked confused, and Rose's irritation drowned out that little speck of guilt. "Look, if it was the other way round, if I really wanted kids and Harley didn't, the baby would still be on its way, and we'd still have broken up. The only reason people are having a problem with getting their heads around this concept is because no one can imagine a woman not going bloody mushy over a baby and a man not running for the hills at the first sign of fatherhood."

"Oh," said Andrea quietly.

"Yeah," she said, and pushed past her colleague to knock on the boss's door.

"Hi, Helen. I need to fill out the paperwork for maternity leave," she said, slumping in the chair.

Her boss glared at her over the top of her glasses. "So I hear." She went back to writing, her pen pressing hard enough on the schedule to warp the paper.

Rose raised her eyebrows. "I don't need long. I thought a few weeks before the due date just in case and a couple of days after to recover."

Helen sighed deeply, tore herself away from her desk to pick up a sheaf of papers already on the printer, and slapped them down in front of her. "Bring them back when you're done."

"Okay," said Rose, drawing out the last syllable, the slight ribbon of anxiety, of "What did I do wrong?" turning into an angry "What crawled up your backside and died?" But she left with a deliberately cheery "Bye."

She was stabbing at her computer, entering the hybridisation data in the profiler when a woman in her thirties from the *Xenopus laevis* department crouched next to her. "How did it go with Helen?"

"Fine," she said cautiously, giving her the side-eye. "Steph, isn't it?"

"Yeah, sorry. Hi. I heard about the baby. Congrats, by the way. I wanted to come over and sympathise when I saw you coming out of her office with the paperwork and intent to kill written all over your face."

Rose cracked a grin. "You sound like you're talking from experience."

She rolled her eyes. "I've got two little boys at home.

Helen and I got along fine until I got pregnant, then suddenly, I'm shit on her shoe."

"Fan-bloody-tastic." Rose groaned. "Has she got a problem with kids? She does know we're not going to bring them in, right?"

Steph smiled sadly, her eyes flickering to the boss-lady's closed door. "It's not like that," she said. "She's been trying to have kids of her own for years. Two cycles of IVF." She looked back at Rose. "Don't spread it around, would you? Someone else told me when I got pregnant with my first, and I haven't told anyone else. I just wanted to pass it on, so you don't take it personally."

"It's not our fault," muttered Rose, grumpy with the lump of guilt that was gnawing at her.

"No," Steph agreed. "But it's not hers either. Don't say anything, just, I dunno, grin and bear it if she's a little catty, yeah?"

"Okay," Rose said. "But I reserve the right to snarl and fight if she's a lot catty."

Steph winked at her and ran back to her station.

"Dear God," prayed Rose under her breath. "Your sense of humour is not even remotely appreciated. Amen."

Chapter Sixteen

Angry

Andrea was trying, Rose reminded herself. Unfortunately, the less accommodating part of herself agreed that yes, she was very trying.

It wasn't very fair on the poor girl. She'd been really thoughtful to notice Rose was no longer going out with the band every night. She'd probably seen Facebook pictures of gigs and festivals with a notable absence of any of Rose. Instead, Rose had spent three weeks of dull, sleepy evenings in her flat wondering how she could have fifty-odd free channels and still be unable to find anything worth watching.

So when Andrea had invited her out for mocktails with some of the other lab rats, she'd jumped at the chance. Sure, she'd had social interaction, but it had mostly been limited to texting Max and Jamie while they worked the fields between Oxford and Whitney. And every time she'd caught herself flirting with Max, and him flirting back, she'd had to take a deep breath and put her phone to one side.

The foetus wriggled like a caterpillar, squirming deep in her gut. She thought of the gig in Jericho, Max kissing some girl, and how if she hadn't been so bitter, she might have had the sense to say no to Harley and go home alone that night.

So mocktails with Andrea, David, and Lily seemed like a great idea. Unfortunately, she'd underestimated Andrea's obsession with gossip. She'd gone out hoping for some distraction, and all anyone had wanted to talk about was the drama still playing out on Facebook, explanations for all the mean comments made about her by people they didn't even know.

"You know there's a reason I deleted Facebook, right?" she snapped when Andrea read out one of Frank's posts and asked her what his problem was.

"Sorry, Rose." She looked taken aback, as if she'd missed all of Rose's snappish replies and darkening mood. "I'm on your side. I thought you might want to have a bit of a rant about them."

"Well, I don't." She grunted. "Are we going dancing or not?"

"Are you sure you'll be okay dancing in your condition?" asked David.

"I'm pregnant, not dying, David. I still go to my karate class once a week. I think I can handle a bit of clubbing."

But the damage had been done. She was grumpy and wanted a mosh pit, not that she cared for the music, but Andrea led them to some tatty place that played the charts in one room and cheese in the other. She slipped away first chance she got and stomped into the patch of concrete that really didn't deserve the name beer garden.

It was quiet out in the open air, without too many smokers. She took a deep breath and leaned back against the wall with her eyes shut.

Her eyes snapped open as music started up. It certainly didn't sound like something this place would play, a heavy guitar beneath a woman's pure, sweet soprano. There was a big concrete planter in the middle of the courtyard, some straggly palms and ornamental grasses fighting for water and sunlight, and she walked around it to see long legs in black jeans, a blue long-sleeved shirt with the sleeves rolled up to expose wiry forearms. Black wavy hair curling around tanned skin the colour of tea the way Mum used to make it for her, with way too much milk and sugar. "Max?"

He looked up and smiled, but it didn't reach his green eyes. "Hey, Rose. What're you doing in this hellhole?"

Before she could answer, the door thumped open, and a handful of drunk lager lads stumbled out. "Alice. Oi, Alice!"

Rose looked over her shoulder at them and turned back with a snort. "Someone's had too much."

But Max was glaring at the paved floor, jaw muscles clenching under his skin and his fingers white-knuckled around his phone.

"There you are, Alice," one of the men yelled, and the three of them stood in front of Max, practically toe to toe with him. "What are you sulking for? You're supposed to be here for your brother's birthday, and you're playing on your phone back here."

Max grunted. "Observant, you are."

Rose looked between the swaying man and Max and made a few safe assumptions. Drunk boy leered at her. "One of your friends, Alice?"

"Nah," said Rose before Max could answer. She draped an arm around his shoulders before the hurt look could solidify. "I'm Max's girlfriend."

The three blokes looked various stages of confused and disgusted. Max gave Swaying Man a shit-eating grin, and Rose was glad she hadn't overstepped.

Then the ringleader smiled, slow and cruel. "Guess Alice here hasn't told you, but she's a bit lacking in the trouser department."

"Oh, I know exactly what he's got in his pants," Rose purred. "C'mon, Max, let's go home." She pulled him to his feet, linking their fingers.

"Fine, love," said the man, raising both hands in mock surrender. "Didn't take you for a rug muncher."

Max opened his mouth to snap, and Rose pulled him close. "Ignore him, babe. He's just jealous I can tell who's the real man here." She leaned in and pressed her lips to his. Her heart beat faster when his hands found her hips, and she pressed closer, parting her lips and licking into his mouth. If this was the only chance she got to kiss him, she was going to take everything she could get.

The drunk guys had left by the time she resurfaced, eyes opening slowly to fix that memory firmly in her head for future fantasy material. He was still close, bright eyes gazing into hers fiercely, and he pushed her back against the wall, sank his fingers into her hair, and kissed her.

Everything below her waist turned to liquid, and she moaned into his mouth as his tongue flicked around hers. He pulled back with a chuckle. "So I hear pregnant women get exceptionally horny." He rolled his hips into hers, and she could see the smirk at the corner of his lips. "That true?"

"It is for me." She grinned.

"Well, you know what they say about pregnancy cravings."

"Give the bag of hormones whatever she wants?"

"That's the one."

Chapter Seventeen

The Morning After

Rose woke up with the sun blazing in her eyes. It took her a moment of blinking before her memory came back online. Her first instinct was the smile crawling across her face, but she squashed it hard and sat up.

Max's room was just big enough for the single bed. It had been a while since she'd shared one of those. Shelves were packed full of CDs and vinyl albums, a stereo in one corner, and a guitar leaning against the wall. No Max, though. She rubbed her eyes and crossed her legs under the blankets.

The door opened, and Max pushed his way in, a tray of tea things clinking in his hand. He looked up and grinned. "I'm not bringing you breakfast in bed. I just don't know how you take your tea."

"Sensible as always."

He snorted. "Sensible? Don't insult me."

The smile cracked her cool mask, and she chuckled as she took the mug from him and added milk and sugar. Max lowered the tray to the carpet and sipped his own tea with a sigh. Rose brushed fingers across the collar of his shirt. "Dressed already?"

He smirked up at her. "Did we ever actually get *un*dressed?"

She looked down at her own T-shirt from the night before to hide the flush as memories of falling back against the sheets rose up, of pulling at his shirt and hands getting pushed away.

"Not for lack of trying," she said because a tease was always preferable to honesty. She plucked at that undershirt he was wearing again. "You wear too many layers."

He gave a half-smile and looked away. "I guess so." He took a sip of tea and looked up. "The shirt stays on," he said in a rush. "I don't like not wearing it."

Rose shrugged. "Okay."

Max nodded to himself and sat back once more, running his fingers across his records. "Music?"

"Yeah, you have a lot. Why vinyls? They take up so much space."

He shrugged. "I like the sound beneath the music. They always crackle a little, it's like, I dunno, a fire in the background. Feels warmer. And I guess I like the commitment to them. You have to look after them and be close while they're playing, otherwise they keep spinning when the song ends."

"So you like to work for your enjoyment?" She laughed.

He gave her a filthy grin. "You tell me."

She tried to cover a blush by groaning and rolling her eyes. No way was she going to tell him he was right. "Go on, Casanova, put a record on."

"What kind of music do you like?"

She tilted her head to one side. "Tracy Chapman, Norah Jones, Nina Simone. Blues, I guess."

"Blues, huh?" He smiled. "I've got some of those guys, but…" He ran his fingers along the shelf, and with a little "Ah," pulled out a battered record. "My grandpa gave me some of his records, too." He held up the sleeve, which showed a man and a woman sitting on folding metal chairs, smiling at the camera. "Ella and Louis. We can pretend we're slicking back our hair with Brylcreem and having burgers and shakes at a diner."

He carefully slipped the disc out, dropped it onto the turntable and gently, almost reverently, lowered the needle into the first groove. A light piano started up a perky jazz tune, and Ella Fitzgerald sang.

Rose raised an eyebrow and reached for the album cover. "They look a bit like my parents. You know. Apart from the whole skin colour thing." She grinned. "And my dad was bigger than Louis Armstrong in this picture. He must have been quite young here."

"I guess most of the pictures of him were from later." Max shrugged. "This album was from the fifties, so I don't think he was that young." He closed his eyes as the song changed, a peaceful, fireside sound. "I love this one, God. Feels like I could fall asleep right here." He leaned back against the bed, his head flopping back so that his hair spilled over her knee, and shut his eyes. Rose let herself smile and brushed through the strands gently while Ella and Louis sang "Can't We Be Friends."

"I've got to work later today," Max said, opening his eyes to blink up at her.

She gestured with her mug. "Fine, I'll just finish this and I'll be out of your hair."

He sat up, eyes widening. "Oh, no, I didn't mean—"

"Hey, Max. It's okay. I mean, we're not dating."

He looked at her, his mouth slightly open. His face seemed stalled, as if he was deciding what expression to make. She took pity on him and nudged his shoulder with her toe. "C'mon, you know me. I'm not going to be one of those one-night stands who won't take a hint." She forced a laugh and drained her tea, pulling her pants and jeans on under the blanket.

"You don't have to be."

He said it so quietly that she had to check to see if he'd even really spoken. "What?"

He blinked rapidly and sat straight. "I mean…this worked

well. Just this, you know? It doesn't have to be a *one*-night stand." He laughed and rubbed his face. "Sorry. What are words? I mean, if you wanted to do this again..."

She smiled slowly. "You gonna be my pregnant lady booty call?" Something under her ribs squirmed, excited and confused.

He mock glared at her. "We'll be each other's booty call."

"Friends with benefits?"

He considered, then nodded sharply.

"All right, then." If she'd been paler, he'd have seen her blush. She pulled her bra and T-shirt on, smoothing it over her rounding belly. "Long as you don't mind this getting more and more in the way."

He laughed and shoved her hip lightly. Blood buzzing under her skin, she dropped a kiss on his cheek. "C'mon, farmer boy. Give us a lift home?"

His smile crinkled up the skin under his eyes, and he drained his cup and jumped to his feet. "Sure, let me just..." He flicked the record off and lifted it gently off the turntable and into its sleeve.

"I'm gonna..." Rose gestured behind her. "Bathroom?"

"Oh, down the corridor to your left." She nodded and actually gave him a thumbs-up before turning to find the door. Really? A thumbs-up? She lowered her butt onto the loo and groaned into her hands.

Was this a really bad idea? Max was one of the only people she could stand to be around these days, and they were stumbling over their words and giving each other awkward thumbs-up.

She rubbed her temples. She really, really liked him. That was the trouble. It mattered if things went wrong. It wasn't like when she'd gotten together with Harley. She'd never cared what he thought of her, but Max...well, at some point, her being selfish and antisocial and bitchy was going to stop being funny and not enough. Or she was going to be too much, too caustic, too fat, too pregnant. She was going to need—

No. She stamped on the Freudian slip in her own mind. She was going to want too much from him, and he was going to step back. The little voice in the back of her head that had always been too vulnerable gently said that would hurt the most. Being rejected, not being the one to step back. Rose gritted her teeth. She'd have to make sure it never got that far. She didn't need anyone, and she never would.

She fixed her makeup, made a face at the lack of deodorant, then nodded firmly to herself and opened the door.

Max was standing at the bottom of the stairs, playing with his phone. He looked up when she started walking down, and for a moment, before the cocky grin broke out over his face, there was a moment of softness or sadness in his eyes that almost made her miss a step.

"Hey, watch it." He laughed, grabbing her elbow. "You don't have to fall into my arms."

"Shut up," she said, smacking his arm. "My socks slipped on the wood."

He laughed and picked his keys off a side table, pushing the door open into blazing sunshine.

"Wow," Rose said, staring down the valley.

Max looked up. "You saw it last night."

She snorted. "I was distracted by your hands down my pants. It's beautiful here."

The two-story cottage stood at the top of a small ridge. On one side was a set of ugly concrete barns and some sort of silo, but on the other side, the land fell away into rolling Cotswold hills split into fields of green, brown, and almost unnatural yellow, dark hedges outlining them. The heat shimmered over the dry grass of the garden, and as she took a breath of hot air, two little birds chased each other past her shoulder, making her jump.

Max's lips twitched. "Swallows," he said, nodding after them. "They've been nesting in the eaves. Bit late for it, really, but spring started late, so…" He looked at his watch. "Hey, I don't suppose you want to see the farm?"

She looked around in surprise. "I thought you were working later."

He scrunched up his lips. "Yeah, I guess it is a bit late. Some other time, or—"

"I'd like that." She cleared her throat and deliberately looked away from his smile. "Yeah, I've never seen much of the countryside. That'd be nice. Cheers."

"Okay," he said softly. "Uh, right. One taxi to Cowley, coming up."

The little Peugeot puttered up the gravel drive, and Max paused at the gate to check for traffic. Rose cocked her head at the sign. "Crooked Mile Contracting?"

Max grinned and pulled out. "Yeah, Jamie's joke. Because it's run by a couple of queers, nothing straight for miles."

She barked a laugh and clapped a hand over her mouth. "Oh my God, you call yourselves…that?"

"Just taking ownership. Plenty of people happy to throw those words at us, might as well pick them up and use them."

She shook her head, still chuckling. "Hey, though, I thought you said you weren't gay. I mean," She gestured to herself. "Obviously, you're not."

He sighed a little, like it was involuntary. "I'm not gay. Obviously. But queer's a good word to encompass…well, not-cis-het, I guess. And the shit I get for being trans has certain similarities with the shit Jay gets for being gay." He shrugged. "Some people don't like it, that's fine. But Jamie and I do, so…"

"Okay. Learn something new each day."

"Also…" He hesitated. "I mean, I have been in a relationship with a guy. Uh. With Jamie, actually."

Her eyebrows shot up. "But you said—"

"Yeah, I said we're not together. Haven't been for years."

His neck was flushed pink under his tan, and his fingers were tight on the steering wheel. She bit her lip and squeezed his knee. "You know it doesn't, like, bother me, right? It's not even any of my business. I mean, we're not in a relationship."

He seemed to sag slightly and leaned into the turn as they rounded a tight bend. "Yeah. I guess, I mean you're my friend, though, right? Friends talk about this, don't they?"

"Yeah," she said, smiling. "I am."

He nodded, still staring at the road, though it was straight, and there was no traffic. "I mean, I just. Didn't want you to think…" He trailed off and cleared his throat. "It's how I worked out that I definitely only like women. Jamie's the best person in the world, he's kind and loving, and his family supported me when my own wanted nothing to do with me, and even then, I couldn't…it just didn't work. So. Here we are." He chewed his lip for a moment. "Basically, I'm saying I can still be friends with someone after I've slept with them."

He pulled over down the street from Rose's flat and turned in his seat to look at her. He was still fidgeting, his fingers twisted together as he looked up from under his long lashes. "I don't want to stop texting you or hanging out at your flat or calling you from the tractor because I'm bored."

She blinked at him for a moment, then smiled and took his hands. They felt warmer than life itself under her touch. "Then don't. I don't want to lose that either. I mean, I'd rather pretend last night never happened than lose that."

His forehead crinkled. "Uh, I don't want to forget that."

"Yeah, me neither."

"I kinda still want to do that again."

She smirked and pulled him close by his collar. "I think that can be arranged," she murmured against his lips.

His breath hushed out fast. "I can arrange it right here if you're not careful enough."

"I'm known for being reckless, you know."

"Shit," he breathed and kissed her hard.

"What time do you have to be at work?"

"Honestly?" he said, biting her collarbone. "Not now, and I don't care."

"Better come up to my place, then, hadn't you? Because we're still parked right outside Mr Singh's shop, and I'm not going to start walking to Tesco's every time I need milk."

CHAPTER EIGHTEEN

NCT

Rose lay on her back and poked her belly. After a moment, the weird squirming sensation happened. She poked it again, and the foetus moved once more.

It felt like a fat fish, squirming around just under the water. Harley had teared up when she mentioned she could feel it move, but she felt a bit weird about it. Invaded.

She sighed and put Stare at the Sun's album on her phone and plopped it on her round tummy. The sprog's movements slowed down to almost nothing, which Rose always found amusing, considering the song was pretty drum-heavy.

She was just dozing off when the doorbell went, and she startled so hard her phone slipped off onto the floor. She rolled off the sofa and onto her feet, grabbed her bag, and opened the door. "Hey."

"Hi," said Harley, his eyes bright and anxious. Any minute now, he'd start jumping up and down, the nerd. "You ready?"

She nodded and followed him out, down the stairwell to his car. "Where's the Squashed Frog?"

"Oh." He laughed, and rubbed the nape of his neck. "Yeah, I sold her. She was a bit inappropriate."

She stared at him. "You loved that car. You saved for years, you said you always wanted a Lotus. Even if it was beat up and ugly, you—"

"I wanted a kid more," he said. "I just never thought it was possible, so…"

She looked at the very sensible little Volvo. At least it was going to be easier to haul herself in and out. It was also less green.

The drive was awkward. Harley tried to make conversation, but Rose was aware she was doing a pretty bad job of answering his questions. She was trying not to stick to monosyllables, but she wasn't that interested in the difference between Isofix and three-in-one car seats or the benefits of skin-to-skin contact. And she didn't know what kind of food caused the foetus to hiccup. It wasn't like it was eating it directly anyway.

Oh. That was another thing. Harley really didn't like it when she called it the foetus. Or "it."

"They're a baby, not an inanimate object."

"Yeah, okay, but it can't hear me. And I don't know if it's a boy or a girl."

"Use gender neutral pronouns at least, they or them, you know?"

"How is that different?"

"I don't know, it just is. 'It' is for nonliving things. Our baby is already a person."

"*Your* baby."

"Yes," he said, a sharp note entering his voice. "My baby."

She rolled her eyes, but he had a point.

❖

The NCT group was meeting in a village hall just outside Oxford. "Sorry it's not closer," said Harley. "The city ones were already full."

"It's closer for you." She shrugged. "And you're the one who wanted to make parent-friends."

He nodded and bit his lip but didn't say anything. Rose sighed and followed him out of the car.

They were all white couples. Because of course they were. Rose slouched in her seat and gave in to the urge to cross her arms over her belly while Harley got her a cup of tea and introduced himself to the others around the refreshments table.

She turned as someone lowered herself into the next seat with a grunt. "Holy crap, my back hurts," she murmured. "Hi, I'm Melinda."

Rose took the proffered hand. "Rose."

"So how long have you got left on your sentence?" she asked, blue eyes twinkling wickedly.

Rose laughed, startled. "Three months."

Melinda raised an eyebrow. "What, like a full twelve weeks? Oh God, I'm due in eight. Counting down the days already."

"What is it with this counting in weeks thing?" asked Rose. "Literally no other person does that, just pregnant women."

"It's because weeks go faster," she said. "Oh, darling, I love you."

A man with greying hair handed her a cup of tea and a biscuit with a fond smile and lowered himself into the next seat along with a satisfied grunt. Harley arrived with her drink just in time to save Rose from laughing at the pair of them.

A willowy redhead clapped her hands together, and a full six inches of metal bangles jangled on her wrists. "Would everyone like to take a seat, and we'll get started? Lovely. So. Welcome to the Hanford NCT group. I'm Crystabel, and I'll be your facilitator. Oh, are you okay?"

"Fine," gasped Rose, as Harley thumped her on the back. "Just…coughing."

"Here, have a cup of water. Better?"

Rose nodded and gulped and shoved her giggles back down.

"How about we go around the room and introduce ourselves? Let's do names, of course. Then Mums, if you can tell us your due dates, maybe the dads can tell us how long you've been a couple? And one more little fact about yourselves. Let's start here."

Crystabel turned to the woman on her right as she sat. She pushed a pair of black rimmed glasses up her nose and waved. "Hi, everyone. I'm Jane, I'm due on September twenty-seventh and...oh gosh, I don't know. I'm so excited to be a mum."

Her partner linked hands with her, and she squeezed him, pressing her face into his shoulder. "I'm Dan. We've been together for what, sixteen years? Married for twelve. Uhm." He squeezed Jane's leg. "This is our second bout of IVF." He glanced around quickly, then down at their joined hands.

"Congratulations, you two," said Crystabel, clapping and jangling. Nobody else joined in the applause, thankfully. Dan looked just as grateful for that as Rose.

"Hi," said the next guy, tattoo sleeves rippling as he waved. "I'm Sam, and we've been together for six years. Not married. I'm an architect."

"Nadine," said the woman on his right, pushing her immaculate bob behind an ear. "November eighth, and I'm an only child so I have no idea what I'm doing."

The group chuckled. "That's why we're here," said Crystabel earnestly.

"Serenity," said a waif with her hair under a colourful scarf. "My little gift is due on the eighteenth of September, and I'm hoping to have a completely natural birth."

The girl squirming next to her almost hopped out of her seat in excitement. "I'm Divinity. I'm her sister and birth partner. I'm so excited to be an auntie, and I'm so proud of my big sis." She squeezed her bicep and tapped her feet on the floor like a drum roll.

Serenity kissed her head fondly while Rose raised her eyebrows at them. She'd never seen anyone look less like sisters. Serenity was as thin as a rake and dressed in hippie gear to rival Crystabel, while Divinity had super short brown hair and denim shorts on her stocky legs.

"I'm Jason," said the grey-haired man near Rose. "My wife and I have been married for two years, together for eight. She's my second. The first wife was just practice."

His wife laughed and smacked his arm. "Melinda, and at forty-two, I'm officially considered a geriatric mother."

"What?" Rose snorted. Melinda and Nadine both nodded sagely. Rose shook her head. Geriatric in your forties.

"What about you?" asked Crystabel.

She started. "Oh, yeah. Uh, I'm Rose. The baby's due on the fourteenth of October and…" She sat up straighter and set her jaw. "I'm just the surrogate."

"I'm Harley," said Harley before anyone could even move. "And you're not *just* anything. You're giving me a blessing I never thought I'd ever have."

"Hear, hear," said Serenity, and the others all murmured agreement and nodded firmly. Rose blinked and looked at her fingers tightly laced in her lap.

It took her a minute or two to get her focus back after that. There were handouts about birth plans and the stages of labour. Harley took notes and put his hand up to ask questions, and Rose sank farther and farther into her seat. She felt like she took a breath for the first time when Crystabel called a tea break, but then she felt too self-conscious to get up and brave the scrum around the refreshments table.

"You look," said a dry voice from Harley's seat, "like a woman on the edge."

Rose snapped her head to the right. Nadine lowered herself, hand cupping her bump. "Hi," she said with a smirk. "Nadine."

Rose shook her hand and sat up straighter. "Hey. Rose. I'm fine, just a little—"

"Overwhelmed?"

A breath rushed out of her. "God, yes."

Nadine laughed, a surprising giggle that scrunched up the skin over her upturned nose. "Yeah, it's a bit much, isn't it? I mean, I knew NCT had a reputation for being all crunchy granola mums."

Rose snorted. "What now?"

"Crunchy granola mums," she said, her eyes twinkling. "They only eat organic, gluten free, fair-trade, vegan meals, their children are called Magic and Serendipity—"

"And Divinity and Serenity?" suggested Serenity, leaning over Nadine's shoulder.

Nadine went so pale, Rose thought she could see her arteries. "I...I didn't..."

Serenity grinned. "It's okay, Mum was exactly like that. She made excellent granola, too."

Nadine put her head into her hands. "Damn. I'm really sorry, I didn't—"

"It's really not a problem," she said, and Divinity pulled up a couple of chairs, disrupting the neat circle. "Look, I'm sure we've all come in here with our preconceived notions, but we're all in the same boat. Truce?"

Nadine nodded, but she didn't look up.

"Hey, if it helps, I thought you were a high powered execu-bitch when I first saw you," said Divinity.

Rose exploded. She bent over and laughed so hard she cried. Even Nadine started giggling along with her.

"There, you see?" said Serenity as Rose wiped her eyes. "What a bonding exercise. NCT's already doing its job."

"I'm still really sorry," said Nadine. "I never meant to insult anyone. I didn't think."

"It's really fine," said Serenity. "I mean it. We all make assumptions. But now we can get past them and support each other as women were born to do."

Rose shrugged. "I'm in. Long as you guys know I'm not gonna have a baby at the end of this."

Serenity pulled her chair closer and took both of Rose's hands. Rose resisted the impulse to pull away. "You're doing such a wonderful thing," she said, holding Rose's gaze just to make her feel that little bit more awkward. "It's the most selfless thing, helping someone become a parent."

Nadine nodded vigorously. "I know I couldn't do it. This whole experience has been a battle with morning sickness and back pain, but at least I get a baby out of it at the end."

Rose snorted, slightly hysterical. "Oh God, giving the baby to Harley will be my reward. I can't imagine being a mother myself."

Nadine and Serenity glanced at each other, obviously taken aback.

"I mean, I don't think there's anything wrong with motherhood. It's just not for me." She shuddered. "It terrifies me."

"Oh, well, me, too," laughed Serenity, relieved. "I think it scares everyone, but it's the most important job in the world, don't you think?"

Rose smiled and hoped they took that however they wanted. She was beginning to feel like Miho, trying so hard not to offend anyone. It was exhausting. How did she do it?

"So how did you guys meet?" asked Nadine. "Through an agency, or..."

"Uh, no, I met him through the band."

"Oh, so were you and his wife friends?"

"He's not married."

"His girlfriend, then." She giggled.

Rose pinched the bridge of her nose. "Look. I was Harley's girlfriend. Or fuck-buddy, whatever. I got pregnant. I wanted an abortion. Harley asked me to surrogate for him instead."

The women were silent. Serenity's mouth opened and shut, and Nadine's eyebrows almost flew off her face. Rose was torn between the impulse to scream or laugh, but before anyone could make a move, Crystabel clapped her hands and called everyone back to their seats.

Great, she thought, avoiding Harley's gaze as he sat next to her. This was going to be as bad as she'd expected.

CHAPTER NINETEEN

Do Your Research

"Tell me you're free this evening," she said after Harley dropped her home that afternoon.

Max was quiet on the other end of the phone, just the slightest pause. "Yeah, okay. You want to come here?"

"Whatever, I don't care. I need some stress relief." She bit her fingernail angrily and refused to admit she actually just wanted to be with someone who didn't think she was a freak. It was too close to other things she didn't want to admit.

"Yeah. Yeah, okay, I'm on my way home now, I just need…" He paused. "Actually, it's okay. Forget it. Come over whenever."

"You sure?"

"Yeah, I'd like to see you."

She blinked and cleared her throat. "Okay, mate. Be there in fifteen."

She found herself getting butterflies on the way to his place, trying to concentrate on the narrow country lanes while her mind yo-yoed between *you're doing such a wonderful thing* and *I couldn't do it*, and *I'd like to see you.*

When she got out of the car and saw him standing in the doorway, his shirt sleeves rolled up to his elbow, she shoved him up against the wall and kissed him hard. "Distract me," she said. Ordered.

He chuckled and led her upstairs.

❖

"You want to watch a movie or something?" he asked later. He was lying beside her, running his fingers up and down her arm and not looking her in the eye.

Rose hesitated.

"With Jamie, too, I mean," he said hurriedly. "Like we used to. Jamie usually streams something on Saturday nights if we're not too busy."

"Yeah, okay," she said. "Sounds good, a night in with friends."

He pushed up with a soft groan and stretched, then clutched at his ribs under his arm. "Ah, damn."

"You all right?"

"Yeah, I'm fine. Just a twinge."

He still wouldn't meet her eyes, rubbing his chest through the shirt *and* the undershirt he insisted on wearing. Rose shrugged and looked for her clothes on the floor. He was still moving gingerly when she was dressed. "You sure you're okay?"

"Yeah, just a cramp or something. We got a truckload of fertiliser to unload. I think I overdid it a bit."

"Take off your shirt. I'll give you a massage," she said, slapping the bed.

"No." He curled away from her, actually clutching the bloody shirt like she was some sort of pervert for asking.

She raised one eyebrow. "All right then, touchy. Jesus, I won't bother." She snatched her cardi off the floor and pulled it on with sharp movements. He was still sitting there, peering up at her with his hand cupped around his ribs. "Look," she snapped. "If you're not going to accept help, at least stop making such a big deal about it. You want to watch this movie or not?"

"Yeah."

"Well, come on then."

She walked out without waiting for him and bit her lip. She didn't know why she was being so grumpy with him. The baby shifted, and she crinkled her nose up, wondering how much of the churning in her belly was guilt and how much was that wriggly little git.

Jamie was in the kitchen and grinned when he saw her, coming over for a hug and a Continental kiss on each cheek. "Bloody hell, Jamie, anyone would think I haven't seen you in months," she grumbled.

He laughed and turned the heat down on the pasta. "Feels like it. I don't get to see so much of you now you're dating my best mate." He put the back of his hand to his head. "I'm so alone."

"We're not dating," she said, perching on a barstool and choosing a crisp from the packet very carefully. "We're just friends."

He looked at her, his face unreadable, then turned back to the food. "Does he know that?"

She rolled her eyes. "Yeah, Jamie, of course he does. We're adults, for God's sake. We can screw around without it meaning anything."

He didn't reply, and the room fell into an awkward silence until Max arrived. "What's cooking?"

"Spag bol," Jamie said shortly. "Grate the cheese, would you, Max?"

He pulled the cheese and the grater across the table, sitting next to Rose. She watched the muscles move in his forearm for a moment until he sucked in a short breath and pulled his elbow in.

Jamie turned with a frown. "Mate…"

"Don't," he snapped. He stood to grate the rest of it, and

Rose frowned between them, Jamie staring at him helplessly until he finished. He pushed it across the table and went to the sink to wash up the grater.

"Okay," said Jamie softly. "It's ready. You want some?" He jerked his chin at Rose.

"If there's enough?"

Max smiled and handed her a fork. "Jamie always over-caters." He turned to reach up to get plates out of the cupboard and *squeaked*, nearly dropping the heavy crockery.

"Max." Jamie turned off the hob and grabbed his bicep. "Max, please—"

"No," he said, pulling free.

"Please," Jamie begged. "It's been too long, I bloody—"

"I need it," he hissed, glaring at Jamie.

Jamie pressed both hands to his eye sockets. "Mate, it's not healthy. You're going to hurt yourself. You're already hurting yourself."

"What's going on?" Rose frowned from one to the other.

Max looked at Jamie, his eyes wild. "I can't. I need this, Jay, let me…"

"I sent you home because you've been wearing it for three days straight." Jamie's eyes were full of tears. He was screaming at Max like he was terrified. "I know it feels wrong, I know the dysphoria's bad right now—"

"You know nothing," Max yelled. "It's all just been handed to you on a bloody plate, so don't act like you know shit about how I feel."

"Max!" Rose's jaw was hanging open, horrified.

"Are you sleeping with it on again?" Jamie asked, his voice still harsh, but tears streaming down his cheeks.

"Screw you," Max growled.

"What the hell is going on here?" Rose almost shrieked.

"If you can't take care of yourself then I will. Take the bloody binder off."

Max's eyes went terror-wide, and he glanced at Rose.

"Oh, what?" scoffed Jamie. "You think she doesn't know you've got a chest?"

Max looked sick. He turned hateful eyes on Jamie. "Fine," he said, almost in a whisper. "Fine. I hate you."

He shoved past him and stumbled upstairs. Jamie sniffed and wiped his nose with the back of his hand. "Leave it outside your door," he yelled.

"Screw you."

Jamie squeezed his eyes shut and leant on the counter, his head hanging low and his shoulders hunched.

"What the ever-loving Christ, Jamie?" Rose said, her heart still beating fast.

"You know what?" he said, still staring at the worktop. "It's really none of your bloody business."

"What?" She wrinkled her nose.

Jamie raised his red-rimmed eyes to her. "You're just screwing about, aren't you? You don't give a shit about what he actually wants."

"What the—"

"You know how long it's been since his top dysphoria was that bad? Three years. Three bloody years, and then you come along, and what he sees in you I don't even...but he's not even good enough for you to call him your boyfriend, is he?"

A chill swept down Rose's back; guilt, sour and oily. She pushed it away. "What..."

Jamie laughed and stood, wiping his eyes and putting the lid back on the pasta, scraping the grated cheese into a Tupperware. "Of course you don't know what that is. You're not *dating* the trans man, you're just using him for sex, why would you need to do any research? Not like you actually bloody well care for him, is it? Look, could you, like, bugger off, or something? I just…I can't with you. Right now."

Rose picked up her keys with numb fingers and left.

CHAPTER TWENTY

Change

Rose dropped her phone on the duvet and rolled over, staring up at the cloudy night sky out her window. She had been working hard at holding back the guilt, but now it was washing over her like a tidal wave, a solid lump rising at the back of her throat.

She'd never exactly identified as nice. But if pushed, she would probably shrug and say sure, she was a good person. Now, though…

It was like the dam walls had broken. She'd used Harley for sex, made him feel bad every opportunity for asking her to keep the baby, called it "foetus" because she wanted to make it clear how much she hated it.

But all that was pettiness compared with what she'd done to Max. She had tab after tab open on her phone internet browser, all telling her what an insensitive cow she'd been.

There was a knock on her door, which startled her, and she rolled to her feet, frowning. When she opened it, she stood, eyes wide. "Miho?"

"Hi," said Miho, chewing at her bottom lip. "I, um, do you mind?"

"Uh, yeah, sure, come in." Rose let her in, picking up a blanket off the sofa to dump it on the chest under the window, picking up a handful of mugs from the table, and turning in a circle before she realised she was basically flapping. "Tea?"

"Yeah, please."

Miho followed her into the kitchen while she flicked on the kettle. Rose heard her take a deep breath. "I came to apologise."

Rose spun round, mouth open to answer, but no sound came out. She gripped the counter behind her back and gaped.

"I was pissed about something that was really none of my business, and I was so rude, I'm so ashamed of myself. Do you think you can ever forgive me?"

"Miho…" She rubbed her temples and felt the guilt press down on her like Atlas's load. "You really have nothing to apologise for."

"Of course I do," she said, huffing a mirthless laugh. "I yelled at you for leading Harley on, I was rude, I gossiped about you behind your back." She swallowed and actually looked a little sick at herself, and Rose winced, wanting her to shut up and stop being so bloody nice for a change. "Harley's a big boy, he can look after himself. It was none of my business, and I let my own feelings get the better of me."

"God, Miho, please, stop. You are way too nice, honestly." Rose pushed forward as the kettle clicked, turning her back to pour the water. "Everything you said was true. Honestly, I've been doing some soul searching, and I really am a terrible person, you know? You shouldn't be apologising to me."

Miho's big black eyes widened. "What are you talking about? You're not an awful person, Rose, who's been telling you these things?"

Rose snorted. "What, are you gonna go beat someone up for me?" She shook her head. "Do you take milk and sugar?"

"Just milk, please."

"Figures, you're sweet enough, aren't you?"

Miho made a face at her, which made her look even cuter.

"Really," she said. "Who's been telling you you're a horrible person?"

Rose leaned back, crossing one arm over her swelling tummy and sipping her damn decaf tea. "I have. It's just that my behaviour recently, with someone I care about has sort of…well, it's come to my attention, really. I hurt someone."

"Was it Harley?" she asked softly, sitting on one of the breakfast barstools.

Rose laughed sadly. "No. Because honestly, I'm that much of a cow that I didn't really notice I'd been hurting him. Or it was more like I didn't care because…" She sighed and rubbed at her hair. "God, you're going to think so badly of me."

"I won't, honestly."

Rose gritted her teeth and stared into her cup. "I didn't care about him. I didn't care about anyone, really. I never noticed, but I actually just don't care very much about people. So, like, with Harley, I know I hurt him, but it didn't matter that much? It didn't sink in, I guess. But with Max…"

She frowned and cocked her head on one side. Rose closed her eyes and rubbed the bridge of her nose. "Yeah, Max and I, well, we're kind of, not dating, but…"

"You and Max? But you're…" She glanced down at Rose's belly.

Rose raised an eyebrow. "I'm wildly aware. As is Max. But you know women don't actually become celibate when they get pregnant? Shocker."

Miho looked abashed. "Okay, fine, sorry. That was a bit judgey of me."

She groaned. "Miho, really, you're…God, can you be a bitch? For once? You really are too nice."

Miho bit her lip and looked up at her. "Maybe you could give me lessons," she said with a tiny twitch of her lips.

Rose stared at her and burst out laughing. "Oh my God, that. That's what I'm talking about, *yes*." She held out a hand for a high five, which Miho gave, rolling her eyes. "I'm loving it, spicy Miho."

Miho laughed and buried her face in her hands. "Oh man, I was so nervous, I thought you were gonna get mad."

"No, seriously, I'm not kidding," said Rose, still chuckling. "You need to be meaner. You're way too nice for your own good."

"I know this is kinda nosy, but do you want to tell me what happened with you and Max?"

She took a deep breath. For the first time, she was deeply ashamed of how she'd acted. Like she actually cared what people thought of her. She wondered if she could blame her newfound shame on the foetus. "I did not do my research," she said at last.

"Oh, Rose, what did you do?"

"I didn't exactly do anything. I was insensitive. I also didn't know what dysphoria is."

"Wow, there's a lot that could go wrong within that whole..." Miho gestured expansively. "That whole arena. What happened?"

She took a deep breath and held it a moment. "I think I'm not going to go into details, it feels a little bit..."

"Oh, okay."

"Only because he might not want people to know what happened. But suffice to say, Jamie yelled at me, I did that research you told me to do months ago, and now I feel like the worst person alive."

Miho winced. "Well, maybe it's not as bad as you think."

Rose held up a finger. "Uh-uh, no more nice Miho."

She rolled her eyes. "Fine, you're evil incarnate, and everyone hates you."

"Better."

"Seriously, though. I think if you go and apologise, whatever you did, I bet it'll make things easier."

Rose made a face, twisting her lips up.

"Hey, don't knock it. Look how it sorted things out between the two of us."

"I still think you didn't have anything to apologise for. It's me. I screw things up. I didn't realise before, but I do now. I'm kinda toxic, aren't I?"

She shook her head. "Look, it's good to think more critically about yourself and everything, but if you want to actually do something about it, you need to start by making yourself vulnerable. Chelsea's always saying if you really want to help people, you have to ask what they want you to do. You can do that."

Rose snorted. "What does Miss *Made in Chelsea* know about it?"

Miho cocked her head on one side. "Well, she is a mental health nurse."

"What? Is she?" Rose groaned and covered her face with both hands. "See, this is what I mean, my God. I just assumed she was, like, some rich kid with no responsibilities and only half a brain cell on a timeshare with Alicia."

Miho snorted tea out of her nose and coughed violently. "Jesus, Rose. Oh my God, you really thought that?"

Rose winced and nodded.

"Wow, you really are a bitch."

"I'm sorry. I didn't know, I just—"

"Assumed, based on appearance? And what, her nickname?"

"Yeah."

Miho blinked at her, looking a bit startled. "Wow. Okay. Well, for your information, Alicia's a law student, so…"

"Yeah, I think we've established that I'm a terrible person."

"I mean, I'm not sure I should even be advocating you spending any more time with Max, really."

"Look, I'm sorry. I really am. I wasn't always like this, you know? I used to care about people. I used to have friends, but it's like…I can't quite remember what it feels like to be kind. Or to think about what might hurt people's feelings." She swallowed and looked into her tea. "And I don't want to be like that anymore. I know that might be too little, too late, but I don't want to hurt people anymore."

Miho looked over her cup of tea and took a sip. "Then don't," she said softly.

Rose opened her mouth to tell her it wasn't as simple as that, then closed it, and finished her tea.

Chapter Twenty-One

Grumpy mood

Rose was sitting at her laptop when Max called. Her heart turned upside down, but she answered before she had a chance to talk herself out of it. "Hey."

"Hey, Rose," he said, his voice upbeat, casual, as if Saturday night hadn't happened. "How're you doing?"

"I'm fine. What about you? God, I'm so sorry about…are you okay?"

He sucked in a sharp breath, then forced it into a laugh. "Oh, yeah, man." The phone crackled, and she could imagine him scruffing up his hair, flicking it out of his eyes. "I'm so embarrassed about that, I was in such a grumpy mood. So what are you up to this week? Anything?"

"Max…grumpy mood? You can't dismiss it like that. It was really bad. And I didn't help. Are your ribs okay? I'm so sorry I was such a cow about it when you were hurt."

"Rose, just…"

"And I was thinking, maybe we should go back to being friends? Because I'm obviously not very good at this, like, I should have done my research. I was being a selfish bitch, and—"

He barked a laugh, harsh and angry. "Okay, so you don't want to meet up anymore? What, because I have dysphoria sometimes?"

"What? Oh, God, no."

"Because it's not catching or anything. You're not going to, like, turn into a guy because you hang around with me."

"It's not—"

"You know, I'm actually pretty good at dealing with this, but sometimes, well, I'm sorry if it's such a downer when I feel like crap, but—"

"Max, shut up, all right?" she snapped. "Jesus, get back in your box and listen for one minute, will you?"

Max was silent, and her heart sank because she'd just done what she'd been trying not to. So much for trying to be nice. And then Max chuckled. "Oh, there you are. I thought someone had given you a personality transplant or something."

"Oh, sod off."

She could hear him smiling through his words. "No, really, I thought the world had come to an end, you being nice and all."

"I can be nice."

"Sure, when you're acting. When you're not actually being you." He took a deep breath, and Rose realised he must be smoking. "I like you as you are, you know."

"What, being a bitch?" she said softly.

"If you want to put it like that," he said casually. "So honestly, did you really want to stop our arrangement?"

She hesitated. "I don't want to hurt you."

"So you thought you'd decide to what, end half of the fun stuff?"

"I meant, look, I have no idea what I'm doing, all right? I'm grumpy and catty and lazy, and I don't do half as much research as I should."

"Probably because you're doing so much for work."

"Yeah, whatever. But I don't want to cause you pain. Like, mental *or* physical."

"Then how about you listen to me? Look," he said, blowing

out a long breath. She could picture the smoke flooding into the air through his lips. "How about I agree to tell you when you're crossing a line, and you promise to listen to what I need you to, yeah? Don't assume you know what's best for me, just listen."

"Huh," she said. "That's actually pretty much what Miho said."

"She says some sensible things, I guess," he said, the grin audible across the line.

"Are you sure you're all right with things the way they are?" she asked.

"Come on, Rose," he said. "We're adults. We can handle a bit of no-strings sex without getting attached, can't we?"

"Yeah." She nodded. "Absolutely, I mean, it's not like we're in a rom-com or anything. This is real life."

"Exactly. I can screw your brains out without losing my heart."

"Glad to hear it."

He chuckled. "So. You free Wednesday night?"

"Only if you are."

Chapter Twenty-Two

Farmer Boy

Max dumped the phone on her chest and sniggered as she startled awake. "It's for you, sleeping beauty."

She blinked at it, then up at him. "Wha?"

He laughed and finished zipping his overalls up. "The phone? Ringing?"

"Is it?" She picked it up and blinked at the screen. "Oh yeah. Huh." She chucked it beside the bed and closed her eyes. Max laughed. "Shut up. It's disgustingly early. And a Saturday, too."

"It's nine a.m., really not early."

She frowned at him, then at her watch, then back at him. "Why are you still here? Jamie hates me enough without me making you late for work."

He pointed out the window where the rain lashed down, clouds scudding fast behind the rooftops. "I got a text from him last night, didn't notice till this morning. The weather's here to stay for a day or so, we won't be able to do much anyway."

"So why are you even dressed? Come back to bed. You're comfortable."

His smile quirked up at one side. "As much as I hate to disappoint someone who asks so politely, I've still got to fix one of the booms on the sprayer. Weekends don't actually exist for farmers, you know."

She yawned and stretched. "Sucks to be you."

She opened one eye to look at him. He was staring at her, his smirk softened to something else, but as he caught her gaze, he moved again, turning back to check around the room. "You seen my keys?" he asked.

Rose sat up and looked at her hands. "Try the coffee table. You always put them there."

He peered out the door into the living room. "Nice one," he said, grinning back at her. He made as if to step back toward her, and she had a vision of him leaning over to kiss her on the forehead before he left. Instead, he swayed back, dropping her a sloppy salute. "Laters, potaters," he said. "Don't spend all day in bed like a lazy townie, yeah?"

"Sod off, farmer boy," she yelled back. He cackled, and as the door clicked shut behind him, she felt her lips still pulled up into a smile.

Her phone rang again. She groaned and slumped back onto the bed, rubbing at her belly as the foetus squirmed and kicked her in the bladder. "Hello?"

"Hello, Rose?"

"Yes, who's this?"

"It's Serenity," said the voice. "You know, from the NCT group? I hope you don't mind me calling this number. You did put it down on the contact sheet."

Rose frowned, then slapped her forehead. "Serenity, yeah. No, I don't mind, is everything okay?"

"Of course. I wanted to call because, well, I feel like we made you feel a bit unwelcome at the class, and I'd like to get a chance to make a better impression, if you're up for that?"

"Oh, no, that's fine," Rose said, pushing herself up again and tangling her fingers in her hair awkwardly. "You didn't do anything at all, it's fine."

"I don't suppose you'd fancy meeting up for a cup of tea

today? Melinda and I got chatting, and we were talking about getting us all together between classes anyway, since there isn't one this weekend. Jane can't make it, but Nadine says she's keen. So how about two p.m. at the Bell in Hanford?"

Rose scrunched up her face and cursed Harley with all her head. "Yeah," she said between her teeth. "Sounds great."

❖

Rose was planning to give herself a pep talk in the car in the pub car park before running in through the rain, but before she could start, Melinda spotted her and waved. Rose frowned and climbed out of the car, tugging her jacket hood up. "Are you limping?" she asked.

Melinda leaned against the wall and winced, pressing into her hip, her umbrella handle in the crook of her elbow. "Afraid so. My hips aren't happy about this little guy being here, so they've gone on strike. Hurts like hell."

"Why on earth are you walking, then?" Rose demanded, torn between yelling at her some more and carrying her in on her back.

"Oh, you know, can't let these things get you down. If I sat down for the whole nine months, I'd be bored stiff. Come on then, let's find the others," she said and hobbled in, Rose fluttering behind her.

The pub was typical of a twee little Cotswold village like Hanford, with roofs low enough that even Rose felt like she should duck, and dark brown décor that looked like it should smell of woodsmoke and old leather but actually smelled of sickly lavender air freshener. Serenity and Nadine sat at a corner table chatting. To Rose's surprise, they looked like they were actually getting along, and Nadine threw her head back and laughed as Rose and Melinda got closer.

"Here they are," Serenity said, pushing out a chair for Rose as Melinda lowered herself carefully into a wooden bench seat beside Nadine. "I'm so glad you came, Rose," she said, turning every inch of that intense gaze on her.

"Uh, sure," Rose said, flickering her a smile.

Serenity put her hand over Rose's forearm, and Rose wanted to scream and shake it off as if it was a venomous spider. "We're so sorry if we made you feel unwelcome. You absolutely are welcome here, whatever your situation."

Nadine at least had the grace to look embarrassed, but even she nodded. Melinda watched with vague interest. "It's really fine," said Rose. *What do you even do when someone clutches you on the wrist? Are you supposed to reciprocate in some way? What are the social rules for such things?* "I mean, it's not like I'm going to actually be a mum at the end of it like you guys."

"That's no reason why we can't make friends," Melinda said.

"Absolutely." Serenity nodded. "We're all in this together."

"I mean, we're all about to squeeze a small human being out of our bodies. We need all the friends we can get," said Nadine.

Rose snorted and slapped her hand over her mouth. Melinda threw her head back and laughed, and Serenity smiled and sipped her tea as they giggled like schoolgirls. "Please say it exactly like that in front of Crystabel," Serenity said with a mischievous twinkle in her eyes. "I'm sure she'll faint."

"Honestly, has she even had children?" Melinda said, shaking her head. "She seems so sweet and innocent."

"She's got three." Nadine laughed. "One of them's a teenager."

"What?" Rose gaped. "She's barely a teenager herself."

"She's forty-three," Serenity said.

"No," Rose said. "God, I hope I look that young at forty-three."

"I don't," said Serenity thoughtfully. "I want to look like an old wise woman."

Nadine snorted. "You're already wearing the right kind of clothing for it. You sure you don't have a crystal ball tucked away somewhere?" She pointed up at Serenity's headscarf, a silky brown and gold thing.

Serenity patted her scarf. "Not a crystal ball, just a rather bald head. Alopecia, you see."

Nadine closed her eyes. "Jesus, someone please surgically remove the foot from my mouth?"

Serenity squeezed her hand, and Rose was glad it wasn't her this time. "I'm not at all offended. I'm not embarrassed by it either, so you shouldn't be."

"No," sighed Nadine. "No, I probably should be. I mean, that's why we're here, right? To say sorry for being judgy with Rose? I really shouldn't make so many assumptions about the way people look. Sorry, Serenity."

Serenity smiled and patted her. "It's quite all right." She sat back and looked around. "Isn't this wonderful? We're all growing and changing so much. I knew this would be a really transformative experience."

Rose sipped her lemonade and kept her mouth shut. She wondered if there was a god somewhere up there really trying to hammer the idea home about being a better person or something because bloody hell, they were really starting to belabour the point here.

❖

If she was going to turn over a new leaf and try to be more thoughtful about people, Rose figured she'd better start with the person growing in her uterus. "Hey, kid," she said, looking awkwardly at the bump. "Uh, how's it going?"

The bump stayed still. Which was unusual, considering how it had been kicking her cervix all the previous night, and wasn't *that* a fun experience that never got mentioned in the movies? Rose flopped back and stared at the ceiling instead. "Ah, just listen to your dad's EP instead." She flicked the music player open on her phone and laid it facedown on the bump as the opening chords of "Diamond Eyes" played.

The music dropped out as a call came through, Max's name flashing up on the screen. The baby must have kicked then, or else something weird was going on with her chest. Maybe hiccups. "Hey," she said.

"Mornin'."

"It's, like, midday, man."

"Then why do you sound like you just got out of bed?"

"Cheeky bugger." She laughed. "Because I'm a vast whale who doesn't need to get out of bed?"

"Oh, are you getting to that really hilarious stereotypical pregnant woman stage where you hate your entire body and everything about yourself and call the baby-daddy names?"

"I call Harley names all the time. This is completely unrelated."

"Genuinely?" he asked. "Because you call me names constantly, but Harley, really? Doesn't he, like, get upset?"

"I don't call him mean names," she said. "You weren't supposed to take it that seriously. Like, I don't go around calling him shithead willy-nilly."

"Willy-nilly, great word. If you're eighty."

"I have the knees of an eighty-year-old, does that count?"

"Absolutely. So anyway, what are you up to today?"

"My schedule is chock-full of heating up some tinned soup for lunch, staring at my toes and memorising what they look like for when my belly gets so big I can't see them, watching crap telly, and maybe, just maybe, downloading a couple of papers about a gene called Indian hedgehog."

Max snorted and started giggling. Rose smirked. Every time Max started asking a question, he'd peal off into more laughter, his voice getting higher and higher. "You okay there?"

"Fine, fine, just crashed a tractor, but I'm totally fine." He giggled again. The thought slipped through before she could stop it that he was utterly adorable. "Indian hedgehog? Are you serious?"

"Dead serious. It's involved in development. We're about to start mapping its activation throughout the different stages of frog embryo growth, so I've got to read up on it. There's a whole family of hedgehog genes."

He snorted and started giggling again. Rose's cheeks were aching with the smile stretching across her face. "Why hedgehog? Just why?"

She laughed as well. "Flies with hedgehog mutations look kinda hedgehoggy? I mean, I personally think they look like sea urchins, but yeah. There's another one called Sonic hedgehog, that's actually much better known."

Max burst into laughter again. "I thought scientists were all sensible and stuff."

"We really, really aren't. Any of us."

"You're spoiling all my illusions here." He chuckled. Something beeped in the background, a whirring noise as he drove the tractor around. "So if you're so busy reading about mutant hedgehogs, I guess you won't want to come visit me in a field."

She snorted. "Why a field?"

"Eh, well. It's a lovely day. There's deer around this area sometimes and buzzards. And I think I saw a hare. Oh yeah, and I forgot my lunch."

She laughed. "What exactly has that got to do with anything?"

"Well, I was thinking you might want to bring your best mate some food? And in exchange, I'll give you a tractor ride."

He drew out the last words in a sing-song voice like he was trying to tempt a small child into doing something, and she laughed at him again. But her stomach, or her chest, or some part of her was twisting up at the idea of him being her best friend. She blamed it on the foetus again. "Oh, go on, then." She sighed. "What do you want? I'll stop by the co-op."

"Aw, yes," he crowed. "Anything you like is good for me. Anything but sausage rolls, though. I've had those like five days running. I'm sick of the damn things."

She shoved herself to her feet. "I'll put on a feast for you," she said, struggling to keep her balance with her constantly changing centre of gravity. "A smorgasbord."

"Smorgasbord," he repeated in an awful accent. "*Das ist gut, ja?*"

"*Das ist* German, idiot." She grinned. "Where are you, then? How am I going to find you, just look for the big yellow tractor?"

"Green tractor, actually, and I'll drop a pin for you and send you my location. Call me when you get to the gates, and I'll give you directions through the farmyard."

"See you in a bit, then," she said, and rang off.

Driving across a dusty yard half an hour later, she rang Max through her hands-free kit. It felt strange driving onto someone else's property, even stranger to turn into a gateway down a dirt track in her little Fiat. The wheel tracks were rough and dry, and the ridge of higher ground between them was thick with grass. The late August sunshine was beating down from a cloudless sky, making a heat-haze shimmer above the drying wheat or barley growing in the field beside her, and she was struck with a visceral sense memory of heat and sea breeze. She frowned and tried to chase it, but that seemed to be the full extent of it. She had so few memories of Timor Leste before they left. She couldn't even really remember what their house had looked like.

She drove the car down a steep slope, keeping to first gear in places as the track undulated under her wheels, more used to taking tractors and four-by-fours than foolish townies in cute little cars. At Max's instruction, she pulled up under a sprawling maple at one of the boundaries and pushed herself out of the car, waving at the tractor.

Max didn't come over straight away, making one final circuit of the field before pulling up to her with a massive roaring engine and a cloud of dust. "How's it going?" he yelled, clumping down the metal ladder between the wheels in his heavy work boots. "Found the place okay, then."

"Obviously," she said, crossing her arms and pretending that he didn't look like sex on legs in a rare short-sleeved T-shirt.

He stuck his tongue out. "What did you bring me? I'm starving."

"It's only just gone midday." She laughed but pulled the bags out of the back seat.

"Yeah, well some of us have been up since six o'clock. Oh, this looks amazing. Wait there." He ran back to his tractor and jumped up the steps, grabbing out a checked blanket and a battered bag. "Where do you want to sit?"

"You have a picnic blanket lying around in your tractor cab, huh?"

"Yes, I carry it with me everywhere. All farmers do, don't you know this about us?"

She made a face at him, but he wasn't looking at her, concentrating on spreading it out near a pretty flowering bush in the hedgerow and running back to take the bags from her. "I've still got some coffee from this morning, you want some? You'll have to share a cup. I hope you don't mind."

"I think if you've got cooties, I've already caught them," she said dryly and helped him pull out the food. Looking at it now, she'd gone a bit overboard. She'd stood in the shop, thinking of all the things Max might like to eat and couldn't resist buying stupid things like antipasti and coated popcorn and—

"Oh my God." He laughed, pulling out a packet of teddy bear shaped ham. "I can't believe you actually got this stuff. I've always wondered if it tastes as heinous as it looks. Do you make a habit of this?"

She grinned, basking in his amusement. "Absolutely not. In fact, I probably shouldn't even be in the same room as that stuff if I'm going to be a responsible brood mare. The NCT people are always going on about preservatives in food."

"Good thing you're not in a room at all, then." He tore into the packet. "Oh my life, it's worse than it looks on the packaging. Look at this." He held up a limp piece of meat, two shades of pink reconstituted ham pressed into the vaguely menacing shape of a teddy. "I swear this is possessed." He rolled it up and shoved the whole thing in his mouth in one go. "It's disgusting," he said, delighted.

"*You're* disgusting. You're lucky I'm not in my first trimester, or I'd be puking all over you right now."

"How far along are you?" he asked, nodding at her stomach.

"Only seven months." She groaned. "Still got ages left."

"At least you're past the three-quarter waypoint."

"Well, not really. Not if you count in weeks, which is, apparently, the norm among pregnant women and literally nobody else. What is that? Every time I count in months, the

NCT women look at me blankly like they've forgotten the entire concept and can't think in anything other than weeks."

"Still not enjoying it, then?" he asked, popping an olive in his mouth. "This is very posh, by the way, thank you."

She smiled at him, ignoring the warm feeling in her chest. It was a warm day, after all. "You're welcome. And no. It's not really about enjoying it. I'm just doing it because Harley is a soft git and wants to make Mum-friends. Jesus, he should definitely have been born a girl."

"I'll be sure to offer him my uterus when I see him next," said Max coolly.

"Oh God." She groaned and smacked her palm onto her forehead. "I'm sorry."

"You should be," he said, his jaw jutting a little. "That was mean as hell."

"All right, calm down," she said, glaring at him. "I forgot who I was talking to, that's all."

"That's not even what you should be sorry about," he said, putting the packet of olives down and meeting her eye at last, exasperated. "I meant that was mean to Harley, not me. Why would you say he *should have been born a girl* like it's such a *bad* thing? Don't you like being a woman? Are women so pathetic that you use your own existence as an insult to a man when he's just trying to be a good father?"

Rose felt her face burning with a cocktail of shame and anger. "Seriously? Are you mansplaining feminism to me now?"

They glared at each other a moment. Max twisted his lips and looked down first. "Yeah, okay, that was…"

"Too much? Stroppy? Good view on the high horse there?"

"Shut up," he said, shoving her shoulder. "I was going to say you struck a nerve there, but that wasn't your fault. Sorry."

"Apology accepted, then." Rose smiled at him and picked at her scotch egg. "And okay, I guess you had a bit of a point."

"Oh yeah?" he said with a grin. "A teeny tiny bit of a point?"

She held up a finger and thumb close together. "That sort of size," she said. She bit her lip, fighting through the shell of cynicism, just a little. "I am trying, you know. I don't want to hurt people any more. I don't know why, but it hasn't mattered to me for so long, what other people think of me, how they're affected by my words. And now…"

He leaned over and kissed her on the corner of her mouth, and she closed her eyes, leaning into it. "I know you're trying," he said, jumping up. "Very trying." He winked and held out his hand.

She smacked his knee. "Cheeky sod." But she took his hand and let him haul her up into his arms. "What are we doing? Are you done with lunch?"

He nodded, holding her waist. The sun came through the leaves and dappled on his skin, tiny spotlights on his nose, his cheekbones, his freckles. "Thought you might like a ride on the tractor."

"I'd rather have a ride on you." She smirked, trying to bring it back to territory she recognised.

He leered at her. "Like that, is it? If I'd known you were up for a bit of *al fresco* dining, I'd have invited you along to a field that doesn't have a public footpath through the middle of it."

She laughed, tipping her head back, drunk on the August heat and the sun and the arms around her waist. "God, we'd traumatise some poor dog walker for life."

He grinned wide and swung her around. "Let's not do that today, then."

"You'll have to take me out farming some other day."

He smiled down at her, his expression softening. She poked him in the stomach and ran up to the tractor ladder, climbing up ahead of him.

The little seat beside the driver's was just wide enough for her to sit comfortably, looking straight down at the complete glass front. Max started up the engine, leaned back to check the machine was digging into the dirt at the right depth, and moved forward along the tramlines. Rose stayed twisted around, watching the soil turn up and over like the wake of a boat.

They had to talk loudly, but even with the noise and the wide-open space, it felt intimate. Max pointed out buzzards and rabbits and some deer walking lazily from one field to another. He explained how to tell the difference between rabbits and the hare he spotted running halfway down the hill, but Rose wasn't even sure she could see anything. She only realised she'd been smiling the whole time when her cheeks started to ache.

Max pulled up to the corner by her car after the field had turned completely brown behind the cultivator. "I'd better let you out here," he said, turning off the engine so the silence echoed in her ears. "I'm moving on to the next field on the list, which is over the other side, quite a trek back to your car."

He climbed out first, then put his hands on her bum, pretending to help her down the ladder, and she laughed and leaned back against him, threatening to crush him. He wrapped his arms around her waist and lifted her down, shrieking.

"If you're going to be out working a bit longer, why don't you keep the rest of the picnic?" she asked, holding out the bag.

"Ah, thanks, if you don't mind?"

She shook her head. "I bought the ridiculous ham for you, after all."

"So thoughtful," he murmured, leaning in to push her against the car and kiss her. She closed her eyes and let the rush flood through her body, drawing it out. When he pulled back, he was flushed, his green eyes dark. "Thanks for coming to meet me. I had a good time."

"Yeah, so did I."

The slightest wind rustled through the leaves, making the spots of light coming through the maple leaves dance over his face. He smiled softly, nudged his nose against hers and kissed her again, softly. "See you soon, mate."

She watched him climb the ladder again, waved as he drove off along the field boundary and around to the next one before she climbed into her car. She was still smiling.

Chapter Twenty-Three

Panic

By the time she got home, she was panicking. She dug her fingers into her hair, tangled from the wind and the dry heat, and pulled.

She rang Miho as she was stumbling up the stairs. "A picnic in a field, that's, like, purely romantic, right? Did I just go on a date?"

"Rose?"

"Yes, Miho, you have caller ID, of course it's Rose. Shit. *Shit.* I think I just went on a date, and I didn't even bloody notice, God, I'm such an idiot."

"Rose, why are you stressing out? Isn't a date a nice thing?"

"I do not do dates, Miho. I don't. In case you noticed, the last time I had a boyfriend, I screwed everything up for everyone. Me and dating is a terrible idea."

There was quiet on the end of the line. "Okay, I'm coming over. Uh, Chelsea's here, can she come?"

"Why are you coming over? What's wrong, is everything all right?"

"Because you're panicking, obviously?"

"Don't be daft, I'm fine. I'll see you later."

"Rose, you're not fine, I can hear you thumping things about in your kitchen. I assume it's your kitchen. Are you at home?"

"Yeah, why?"

"Because Chelsea and I are coming over, hang tight, okay?"

She frowned at her phone and shoved it in her pocket, bustling from place to place in her flat, throwing things into cupboards, shoving dirty dishes into the sink, anything to keep herself moving and not think, not stop to remember Max's soft lips, his smirk that turned into a sweet smile, his arms wrapped around her, spinning her, just for fun, nothing more.

Damn it. She clutched at her hair, pulling until it hurt to try to dispel the thoughts because she couldn't go down this road again, she just couldn't.

The doorbell rang, and Rose swung the door open, harsh and glaring. Miho looked up, her eyebrows up. "Uh, you okay there, Rose? You look like you're about to murder someone."

"Ugh," she answered, stomping into the flat and throwing herself onto the sofa. The door shut behind Miho as she and Chelsea moved closer.

Chelsea held out a bottle of fizzy grape juice. "Hey."

Rose peered at her. "So you don't hate me anymore either?"

Chelsea shrugged. "I'm reserving judgement," she said. "I think you used Harley, which isn't cool. You knew how he felt about you, and you slept with him because he was easy?"

Rose made a face and looked away. "You make it sound like a conscious decision."

"And you make it sound like you had no control over it," Chelsea said, raising one eyebrow.

Miho brought over a trio of wine glasses. "Now, what's this about Max? You weren't making any sense on the phone."

Rose sighed and tried to put her thoughts in order. "So a few months ago, we started…"

"A relationship?" Chelsea said, her eyebrows shooting up into her artfully messy hair. "Damn, that's fast."

"No, not a relationship." Rose frowned. "Friends with benefits. We were both horny, and I guess, well, I'd actually started thinking about what it might do to Harley to stay with him. I just wanted to have fun, you know?"

Chelsea glanced at Miho, nodded at her, *I know, right?* written all over her face. "Seriously, how do some women jump from relationship to relationship?" Chelsea groaned. "My dry spell's lasted over three years now, and you're still getting no-strings sex while pregnant." She shook her head and drank. "I fail to see what the problem is."

Rose swirled her drink around the cup, listening to the fizz rise and fall with the movement. "Well, I think there might be…strings, now."

"Oh, Rose," Miho yelled, looking furious.

Rose raised an eyebrow. It was like being yelled at by a kitten. "What?"

"It wasn't enough for you to mess Harley up, you had to mess with Max's heart as well? What the hell?"

"It's not like that," she snapped. Then sat, covering her face because it kind of was, wasn't it? "Oh, God." She groaned. "Why do I keep hurting people?"

Miho drained her drink and stood, stomping out of the room. For a moment Rose thought she might have left, and it made her chest feel strangely hollow. But the kettle flicked on, and she started thumping around with cupboard doors. Rose dug her fingertips into her eye sockets and wished she could stop caring again, wished she could find that detachment she'd been so used to.

"Why do you keep hurting people?" Chelsea asked, and when Rose opened her eyes, she was leaning forward, looking at her seriously. Rose hadn't known she had a serious face. "Why do you keep going for the same relationships, what's that pattern all about?"

"Are you psychoanalyzing me?" she asked dryly.

"Are you deflecting?" asked Chelsea with a quick grin. "Look, all I'm saying is, there's got to be a reason why you push people away as soon as they get close."

"I'm not pushing you away."

"And I'm not that close. But when your relationship with Harley broke down, you managed to alienate most of the Sunbirds, too. And now Max."

"And Jamie. And Andrea at work," Rose murmured, drinking her grape juice and wishing desperately for it to be absinthe or something that would take it all away, just for a little while.

"When was the last time you had a proper relationship? Not like with Harley, where you knew you didn't actually love him. When was the last time you loved someone?"

Rose stared at the door, thinking back, trying to remember. She turned her head slightly to look at the photo. "Last people I really loved were my mum and dad," she said softly, and closed her eyes, feeling overwhelmingly sad and alone. "Christ, that's depressing."

The other side of the couch shifted, and she opened her eyes to Miho holding out a cup of tea. "It's decaf," she said, a sympathetic little smile on her face.

Rose sighed and took the cup. "Cheers."

"Is this them?" Chelsea asked, standing to look at the photo.

"Yeah." Rose couldn't help the smile that crept across her face any time she looked at the picture. Mum's laugh had been infectious, and Dad had worn his love for her written across every line on his face when he looked her way. They'd been so happy. What would they think of her now?

"When did they die?" asked Miho softly, putting her hand on Rose's knee.

Rose cleared her throat. "In my second year of uni. Car crash."

Miho squeezed her knee, and she wanted to pull away, push the two girls out the door, and stop them from pulling this vulnerability out into the open. Close off, close the lid on the memories, and shore up her walls, strong and unbreakable.

"Have you got any other family?" Chelsea asked, coming to sit back on her bean bag and looking at her with a kind of respectful kindness. It was easier to look at her than at Miho, who looked like she was going to cry on her behalf. There was something of a blank slate on Chelsea's face, as if she didn't expect Rose to feel any particular way. She was waiting for whatever came her way.

Rose shook her head. "Not in the UK. I actually don't know if there's anyone…we left Timor Leste before independence. I must have been seven." She stared back at the photo. "I had a brother," she said softly. "He died in the violence."

"Oh, God, Rose, I'm so sorry," Miho said, sniffling.

"Are you crying?" She laughed. "Oh, bless your soft heart, Miho, you're so silly. It was years ago. I barely even knew him. And at least the rest of us survived and got out together. There was some awful stuff in the camps before the evacuation." She shuddered. "We were lucky, really."

"And you've never loved anyone since then? Since losing your entire family? You don't think that's probably got something to do with it, some unresolved grief issues?"

Rose glared at Chelsea. "Oh, stop with your mental health nursing. I told you not to psychoanalyze me."

"No, you didn't." She grinned. "You asked me if I was psychoanalyzing you. And anyway, it's worth thinking about."

"Come on. You're saying that me not being able to have a healthy relationship is all because of my childhood? I had a fantastic childhood. My parents were amazing. And an incredible example of a healthy relationship, too. They adored each other. And me."

"Not just your childhood, but the death of your parents. You've lost everyone, Rose. Everyone you ever loved."

"Oh, gee, thanks."

"No, it's horrible. I'm not saying it to be mean, I'm saying that you've experienced some really traumatic things, you must have seen terrible things in Timor Leste, and I doubt you've processed your grief either. Don't you think you might need some help with that?"

"I'm not going to a shrink to talk about my feelings." She snorted. "God, I couldn't imagine anything worse. I want to kick you two out bad enough."

Chelsea made a dismissive gesture at Rose. "Fine. I'm not your therapist. You probably wouldn't even count me among your friends, would you? No, don't answer that. I'm not fishing or anything. But I am starving. How about I pop down to the noodle place and pick us something up?"

"Now you're talking my language."

CHAPTER TWENTY-FOUR

Choices

Rose wanted to throw herself onto the bed beside Max. Instead she had to lower herself down, one hand pressed against her belly, the other holding her up. Max, the git, laughed at her. "Shut up," she grumbled, and shoved herself backward. "I cannot do anything right now. I swear to God, my body has been invaded and is losing the siege."

He poked her belly and watched as the foetus squirmed, shoving up against her diaphragm. She grunted and wished she could shove it back. "Seriously, I've still got over a month to go before I get rid of this little freeloader. How can I possibly get any bigger?"

"You're not actually big for a pregnant lady," he pointed out.

"That's true. Serenity, one of the girls in my NCT class, she's absolutely huge. And she's this tiny little waif as well. She's vegan, though. How can the baby possibly thrive on that sort of diet?"

"Beats me. I'm nothing without bacon."

"I know, right?" She grimaced and shifted onto her side. "Pass me that pillow, would you? My hips ache." She shoved the pillow between her knees.

"Classy." He grinned.

She gave him the finger. "When you grow an interloper in your body, you can talk."

"Yeah, not gonna happen."

"I thought not." She sighed. "I never thought I'd have an actual baby growing in my actual body. It's like an alien. All the other NCT mums keep talking about how they already love it, and I wonder what's wrong with me, you know? Nadine actually said she was going to be a little bit sad to give birth because she wouldn't have the baby safe inside her all the time, and I thought she was the sensible one."

"I can't relate," he said, an amused grin twisting his lips.

"Yeah, well, me neither. Kinda makes me wonder. Am I broken or something?"

He looked to the ceiling, settling himself comfortably on the bed next to her and clasping his fingers together over his stomach. "I don't think so. Everyone says that mums are hardwired to love their baby the moment they get pregnant, and you know, I don't think that's true. I think lots of mums are excited. I do believe lots of mums fall in love with their baby the moment they get pregnant. They're happy to have them there. Even people who weren't expecting to have a baby, even if they're also crapping themselves about the whole experience, and they don't feel ready or whatever, but I don't think it's an automatic, guaranteed thing." He turned his head to the side. "I think loving someone—loving anyone—is a choice, to a certain extent."

She frowned. "You think? Even parental love? You don't think that's different? I mean, of course you choose to love, like, a partner or something, but I've always thought that a parent's love for a child is automatic."

He snorted and looked out her window, stretching his arm back behind his head. "Maybe that's how it was for you. That's cool."

She lay there, watching him for a moment, thinking about

all she knew of him. She poked him in the elbow. "Go on. Tell me your theory. I've never really thought about it that much, and it looks like you have."

He carried on staring out at the cold September sky. "I don't know. I haven't exactly thought about it a lot either, you know. Or at least, not from this end of the equation. But it seems to me, like, a lot of parents, well, they can at least make the choice to *not* love their child, can't they?" He turned to look at her at last. "I think a parent does choose to love their kid, just as much as a person can choose to love a partner. Think about Harley. He's chosen to become a single father. He's chosen to be really excited about this, to alienate half his friends because having the baby is going to make things difficult for the band."

"But that's actions, that's things you do *for* love, not the other way around."

"Are you so sure?" he asked, rolling over so his knees nudged against hers. "Say someone tells a person every day that they're disgusting, that they're attention seeking and pathetic. Say they force a person to dress a certain way because *you're showing me up, you're embarrassing me*. And then one day, they decide the best way to turn that person into someone they want to be associated with is to cut all ties with them, turn them out with nothing, and say *you can only come back when you accept my truth.* And yet, they tell everyone else that it's all done for love."

"That's not love," Rose said softly.

"And what's the difference? How can you know that's not love? They said they loved…that person."

Rose rolled her eyes. "Yeah, I've figured out it's your own story, Max, you don't have to extend the metaphor."

His lips twitched. "You really are a cow, aren't you?"

"I didn't say it wasn't a desperately sad story. I didn't say I don't want to go slap both your parents so freaking hard they forget their own names."

He smiled properly. "You're getting better at this. That was thoughtful, thank you. And it wasn't too nice, either, still very you."

"I try."

He shoved her shoulder. She barely moved, weighed down by her bump. "Anyway, like I was saying," he said, pointing at her. "What's the difference between Harley and my parents? They're both parents. By your definition, my dad should have felt the same automatic, biological love for me that Harley feels for his baby, but can you imagine Harley throwing his child out at seventeen for trying to be themselves?"

She shook her head. "No, thank God. I mean..." She patted the bump. "I don't love the thing, but I don't want any harm to come to it either, you know?"

"Then what's the difference? How does one person's love cause them to reject their child?"

"Yeah, okay," she said, nodding thoughtfully. "I guess I see what you mean. It really is a choice, isn't it? Your parents chose to be arseholes." She frowned, turning her head slightly into her pillow. "My parents chose to love me. God, that feels different. I guess I've always taken their love for granted, but they chose to be good people to me." She smiled up at him.

He smiled down at her, soft, and linked his hand with hers.

Chapter Twenty-Five

Baby Season

"Oh my days." Nadine sighed, slumping in the corner booth of Costa, wincing and straightening up again. "I'm so unbearably uncomfortable, I might have a little cry."

"Feel free." Rose grinned, sipping her decaf latte. "I'll join you."

"I'm posting an eviction notice to this baby," she said, stroking her swollen belly. "I'm so ready to meet them."

"You think it's gonna come before the due date?" Rose asked.

"I have no idea. I'm not one for feelings like that. But I did have a nightmare the other day that I was cooking Christmas dinner for my in-laws, and I was still pregnant. Do you know what a twelve-month pregnant belly looks like? Because my subconscious has some strong opinions on it."

"Oh my God." Rose cackled.

Nadine joined in laughing. "The weirdest thing is, my waters broke as I was taking out the turkey, and I just carried on serving the food. I thought, well, it's not here yet. I guess I'll wait until the dessert course, and then I look down, and there's this little doll-like thing on the floor, waving up at me."

Rose wheezed, hand over her mouth. "You've been watching too much *Monty Python*."

Nadine giggled. "Oh, stop, I'm going to wet myself." She

wiped her eyes. "Have you met Serenity's baby yet? She's gorgeous."

Rose shook her head. "What's its name?"

"You're not going to believe this. It's Mary."

"No."

Nadine nodded, a wicked twinkle in her eye.

Rose tried to imagine it. "I could have sworn she was going to call it Transformation or Chakras or some place name like, I don't know, Outer Hebrides."

Nadine snorted, slapping her hand over her mouth to stop spitting her tea everywhere. "Can you imagine calling your child Hebrides?"

"Absolutely not, but I can imagine her calling her child Hebrides."

"Oh, bless her. We shouldn't be mean."

"I don't think we're being mean. It's nothing Serenity wouldn't say about herself, is it?"

"Yeah, she's a good laugh, that one. Melinda, too, the two of them have become really close, I think."

Rose snorted inelegantly. "Talk about opposites attract."

Nadine cocked her head on one side. "I don't think they're that different, not really. Melinda's a bit of a hippy, you know?"

"Really?" Rose laughed. "I can't imagine her in floaty scarves and long, tie-dyed skirts."

"She's really into crystals and candles, though. You'd be surprised. I went over to see her and baby Robert last week, and she's got incense burning all over the place."

"Ugh, I can't stand that stuff. I hate the smell of it."

"Yeah, I'm with you there." She sipped her tea. "Robert is adorable, though, all scrunched up nose and teeny-tiny fingernails, so cute. He looks so much like Jason, it's unreal."

Rose looked skeptical. "Everyone says that about babies,

but I don't see it. They all look exactly the same. Like they've been deflated."

Nadine laughed, slapping her hand over her mouth again to stop the noise. "Oh my God, deflated babies."

"It's true."

She wiped her eyes. "Hey, did you hear Jane's going in for her C-section tomorrow? I think she's so nervous, bless her. It's been a hard slog for her, just getting pregnant."

Rose screwed up her lips. "Man, life isn't fair. People who want babies have to struggle to get them, and then there's me. I got pregnant completely unplanned, using contraceptives and sleeping with a guy who thought he was infertile."

Nadine's eyes widened. "Wow, that's…you must have super-eggs."

"Well, you're welcome to have the rest of them. I should actually look into egg donation."

Nadine cocked her head again, her bob just brushing her shoulder. "You really don't want kids? Even after feeling this one growing inside you?"

"Not even a little bit," said Rose firmly. "I don't want to be a mother. It never appealed."

"But I think you'd be a great mum."

She laughed. "Don't talk such rubbish. I'm grumpy, selfish, and I genuinely don't care about most people."

"You care about Harley, enough to go through nine months of pregnancy for him."

She twisted her lips. "Meh, I'd only feel guilty if I didn't." She stared into the dregs of her coffee, thinking a little bit deeper than she usually would. "I guess I do care about him. I don't love him, I never did, but he's a good man. And just because I don't want to be a mum doesn't mean I don't understand how passionately he wants to be a dad. He'll be a great father."

Nadine nodded. "Bless him, he's so excited." She shifted a little, trying to get comfortable. "I'm excited, too, you know? I can't wait to meet all our little people." She leaned forward and put her hand over Rose's. "I hope you'll still hang out with us afterward. I know you aren't going to be a parent, but we're all quite fond of you."

Rose smiled awkwardly and wondered why.

CHAPTER TWENTY-SIX

Eviction Notice

"Max," said Rose, getting out of her car and slamming the door. "I'm going to need you to drive me across the bumpiest field you know of, and then we're going to have a curry so spicy, it will set your throat on fire, have a whole pineapple for dessert, and then I'll need—hmm, let me see—three orgasms, I think."

Max stubbed his cigarette out and sniggered. "Hello to you, too. Demanding, aren't you?"

"You'd be demanding too if your own personal space invader was overstaying its welcome. Five days overdue, *five days*. I am not a happy bunny. My back hurts, my ankles are actually swollen—I thought that was a myth—and my bump is so huge, it's making me fall over when I'm not even moving. In fact, I'm about to fall over now, can we go inside please?"

"Well, since you asked so nicely." He grinned and gestured her into the door ahead of him. "Three orgasms, huh?" he murmured as she went past and bit her earlobe. "I think I can handle that."

"Smug," she said, trying to pretend she hadn't just shivered.

"Is it, or is it not, entirely justified?"

She rolled her eyes but didn't deny it. He grinned like the cat that got the canary and pulled her upstairs.

❖

"I was serious about the whole driving across the field thing," she said sleepily, staring at the sunset out his window as he lay on her arm. "It's even frosty now, the ground will be all nice and hard. Really shake this little bugger loose."

"I'm not shaking a baby out of your womb." He grinned. She could feel his cheek stretching against her skin.

"You're no help at all. What about a curry?"

"The last time you had a curry, you nearly cried. I thought you were from Malaysia. Don't you have spicy food there?"

She slapped him on the arm. It made a satisfying noise, and he grumbled at her. "I'm from Timor Leste, you cretin."

"Cretin?"

"At least you didn't say Indonesia. Ugh. I'd have had to kick you out of bed."

"It's my bed."

She poked at her belly. "Yeah, well, someone else is invading my space. Feels right to steal yours."

"That makes no sense whatsoever." He raised his head so she could see his unimpressed expression, then dropped it back onto her shoulder. "You can have a korma. That'll do for you. The baby will come when it comes."

"Easy for you to say. You're not the one who's going to have to expel it through your genitals."

He groaned and laughed. "You have such a way with words. Come on, if you're really serious about the food, I'll order curry, but we'll have to pick it up."

"Nah." She sighed, rolling over awkwardly as he got up and hunted around for his clothes. "It's pointless anyway, you'd have to eat vast quantities of it for it to have any effect. But God, it feels like anything's worth a shot right now."

He smiled sympathetically down at her and offered his hand to help her up.

Jamie was in the living room when they got downstairs and called out to them. "Pizza's in the kitchen."

"Has it got pineapple on it?" called Max.

"Pineapple? Why the bloody hell would it have pineapple?"

Max poked his head through the door to grin at him. "Rose reckons it'll send her into labour."

"I hear orgasms are good for that."

"Yeah, we tried that already," said Max.

Jamie groaned. "Oh, mate, I do not need to know."

"Well, you started it."

Jamie pinched the bridge of his nose. "Go eat your damn pizza, you horrible man."

Max cackled and pulled Rose behind him into the kitchen. "Grab a plate. We'll eat in the sitting room. I think they've got horror movies coming on film four. Maybe we'll scare the little critter out."

She followed him, a piece of pizza already hanging out of her mouth, back into the sitting room. It was still a bit awkward to be around Jamie. She hadn't really spoken to him properly since he'd yelled at her, and both of them were forcing conversation and pretending to be *completely fine, honestly* while not looking each other in the eye.

She'd thought they were doing pretty well, too. They could probably carry out a friendship like this for the rest of their lives. Honestly, it would be more meaningful than half the relationships she'd had in the last ten years.

Obviously, Jamie didn't agree. She'd been lulled into a false sense of security by the time Max went off to have a shower. She'd almost forgotten he was there, and when he sighed and shifted in his chair to face her, she actually startled a little.

"So have you sorted your shit out, Rose?"

She blinked at him. "What?"

He clenched his jaw. She watched the muscles move by his ears. "I mean, I don't want Max getting hurt."

"You know, Max can look after himself."

"I know that," he snapped. "Don't you think I know that, after everything? But that's the thing about being friends, about caring for someone. You don't want them to have to do all that by themselves. Do you actually care about him? Or are you just using him still?"

She bit her lip and turned back to the TV. "I'm not using him, Jamie."

"So are you guys—"

"Look, we're adults," she said, glaring at him. "I told you this before, it's a mutual thing. All we are is friends with benefits. We're not in a relationship, nobody's in love with anybody, nobody's going to get hurt."

"You make it sound like you can't get hurt by friends." He frowned. "Do you really think that, I don't know, giving yourself that stupid name is going to make your relationship safer? Just because you don't call yourself his girlfriend doesn't mean you're protected from feeling, like calling yourself Harley's girlfriend didn't actually make you love him. Did it?"

She turned away, holding her eyes wide, staring fiercely at the light to make the stupid pregnancy hormone tears back off. Eventually, Jamie sighed and took his plate into the kitchen, leaving her alone on the sofa.

Chapter Twenty-Seven

Action Stations

Rose woke up, eyes wide, and raced out of the room naked. She could hear Max grumbling and moving around, but she was absolutely sure she was going to pee right now, and there was no way she wanted to do that in front of him.

She hurled herself into the bathroom and onto the loo, and that was definitely not right. Like…definitely not right.

"Hey," Max croaked from the doorway, rubbing his face and peering at her through eyes still mostly shut. "You okay?"

"I think my waters just broke," she said, staring straight ahead.

There was another gush of liquid, and Max's hand fell away from his face. His jaw hung open. "How much water is in there?"

"I don't know. Melinda said when hers went, it was like she'd wet herself, but this…oh my God, it's going again."

"Shit. Shit, I'm going to call the ambulance. I'm—"

"Max! Don't do that. You call the midwives unit in the hospital, jeez. We don't need an ambulance."

"What do you mean, you don't need an ambulance? We're like fifteen minutes away from the hospital. You're going to give birth."

She stared at him. "Yeah, labour can last up to, like, three days."

He paled and gaped at her. "Three *days*?"

She nodded and grimaced. "Well, they won't let this one go on that long, at least. They said at the NCT meetings that they take it out the sun roof if you're still labouring twenty-four hours after your waters break because of infections."

"Out of the sun roof?"

"Yeah, an emergency C-section. Are you going to repeat everything I say, or are you going to get my phone so I can call the hospital?"

"Shit, yes, I'm going. Are you sure you don't need an ambulance?"

"Max!"

"I'm going."

"And bring my clothes, will you? Don't want to give Jamie a free show."

Jamie yawned from down the corridor. "What are you two doing, thundering around like elephants?"

"Stay out of the bathroom," she yelled. "I'm naked in here."

"Why?"

"She's in labour," said Max, sounding more out of breath than he really should be considering the short distance between the two rooms.

"She's in labour?"

"Oh my God, you two and the repeating everything, jeez. Phone, please, Max."

"Do you need an ambulance?" Jamie squeaked.

Rose growled under her breath and shoved the door shut on the two panicking boys, trying to act like she wasn't terrified herself. Thankfully, the midwife was calm and professional.

She took a deep breath after that and clicked on Harley's name. The phone rang three times. "Rose, are you—"

"Yeah, it's time." She sighed. "My waters broke, but I

haven't started contractions. The midwife said to come in when my contractions have hit five minutes apart."

"Okay," she heard him scrambling around. "I've got the baby's hospital bag here. I'm on my way to your place."

"No, uh. I'm not at my place." She winced. "I'm...I'm at Max's."

There was a pause. "Oh."

Rose squeezed her eyes shut, mortified. "Yeah."

He cleared his throat. "Okay, well, have you got your hospital bag with you?"

"Harley, I don't even have a hospital bag." She slumped slightly, squashing the little, weak part of her that wanted to panic and despair.

Harley sighed, just at the edge of her hearing. "Right. I'll stop by Tesco's and pick some stuff up for you. Do you want me to come there and pick you up when you're ready?"

"No," she said, rubbing her temples. "That's crazy. That's completely in the opposite direction for you. I'll get Max to drop me off, but I'll ring you just before I leave so you know what's going on."

"Sure, no problem. I'll see you there. Just...never mind. I'll see you there."

She hung up and sat with her head in her hands for a moment. "Right. Get up, Pereira." She shook herself off, squashed down the humiliation, and by the time she'd had a quick shower and wriggled her clothes back on, she felt ready to face the inquisition.

Both boys were standing, staring at the door with one arm crossed over their chests and the other bent up to fiddle with their lips. She smirked. "You two spend way too much time with each other."

"Are you all right, Rose?" Max asked, darting forward to hover at her elbow.

"Does it hurt?" asked Jamie.

She frowned. "Actually, no, it doesn't. The contractions haven't started yet."

Max and Jamie glanced at each other. "I was expecting a lot more screaming," Max admitted.

"Don't look at me." Jamie shrugged. "The only experience I have of childbirth is movies."

"But you've got nieces," Max said, waving his hands around in exasperation.

"I wasn't there when they were born, was I?"

Max turned back to Rose. "What do we do now?"

She shrugged. "We wait. They said if the amniotic fluid is clear, then I can hang out at home until my contractions get to about five minutes apart. They told me to go back to bed."

The boys glanced at each other, then back at her. "Uh, do you want to?"

She puffed out a long breath. "I don't think I could sleep right now."

Jamie nodded firmly. "Bacon sarnies it is. Come on, let's go put the kettle on."

Rose took two steps, then groaned. "Oh, man, that's... horrible."

"What? What is it?"

She looked down at hear jeans, now soaking wet. Max burst out laughing. "It looks like you've wet yourself."

"Yeah, yeah, thanks for that. The midwife said some people get like this. Some women get more water than others. I guess I'm one of the lucky ones."

"You know," Jamie said, cocking his head. "It kind of looks like you've shrunk a bit."

"I'm not surprised. I just produced three entire waterfalls."

He chuckled and carried on down the steps. "Come on, off

the carpet. If you're going to keep gushing like that, we'll put some newspaper down for you."

"You know how to make me feel special," she snarked, wincing as her wet jeans rubbed against each other. "Oh, this is disgusting. Sorry, Jamie, you're going to have to put up with me in my pants."

"Don't you bloody dare," yelled Jamie, but she was already peeling the ruined jeans off in the hallway.

"I'll get you my dressing gown," said Max with a grin. "And maybe some towels."

"See, that's why I like him more," said Rose, pointing at Max with a thumb.

"Shut up, you like him more because he's willing to give you orgasms," Jamie said, hands firmly over his eyes.

She nodded. "There is that."

Max sighed. "Good to know my function in life: towels and orgasms."

By the time the bacon was cooking, the contractions had started. At first, they were little waves of pain, like mild period cramps. Max watched her like a hawk, his phone out to time the contractions like she'd shown him. By the time Jamie set the bacon sandwich in front of her, she was pressing her face against the counter, her fists clenched and Max hovering at her back, rubbing her spine.

"Are you okay?" Max asked, his green eyes bigger than ever.

"Don't stop rubbing my back, yeah?" she said, nodding. "God, I really don't want to eat that right now."

"You should," said Jamie, looking at his phone. "It says here you should eat in the early stages so you can keep up your energy levels." But he looked sympathetic.

Rose sighed and shoved a quarter of the sandwich into

her mouth, chewing determinedly, one eye on the timer on Max's phone. They were about seven minutes apart, and she wanted to make sure she didn't start another contraction with her mouth full.

"Can you take anything for the pain?" asked Max, sitting on the stool next to her, his hand still rubbing up and down her back.

"Just paracetamol," she said. "They'll let me have the stronger stuff when I get to the hospital." She looked up at him, and a part of her was lighting up with warning sirens, telling her not to be so vulnerable, not right now, not ever. "Can you drive me in, please?"

He nodded, and she relaxed, taking another bite of bacon sandwich. She barely had time to swallow it before the next wave hit.

The boys subsided to quiet, wincing every time she screwed up her face or swore. Jamie nibbled listlessly at his own sandwich, and Max alternated between rubbing her back and convincing her to eat.

It was five in the morning when Max held up the phone after another wave. "The last three of them have been a little over four minutes apart," he said. "Do you think it's time to head in?"

She took a deep breath and nodded. "Yeah, probably best. I've gotta phone Harley."

Max stopped, a horrified look on his face. "Oh God, I've just realised my car's filthy…"

"In case you hadn't noticed, so am I?" She gestured to her crotch, the towel pressed between her legs already drenched.

"Yeah, but it's not sterile."

Rose rolled her eyes. "I seriously doubt any woman's getting transported in a sterile car. Let me take the last dry towels. It'll be fine, Max."

"Are you sure?"

She gritted her teeth as her belly cramped up, the muscles hardening under her skin, her back bowing. "Yes," she ground out. "I'm bloody sure, now will you please take me to the hospital where they have drugs?"

By the time they reached the maternity ward, she was moaning through every contraction, her body twisting as she tried to somehow escape the pain. She was finding it hard to think, hard to care that she must have looked so weak, so pathetic, and when Max wrapped his arm around her waist to help her into the hospital, she leaned against him, her forehead pressed against his neck.

Harley spotted them as another contraction hit, as she was pressing her face into Max's shoulder, humming a long, wavering high pitched wail. "Rose," he said, running forward, his hands out like he was going to catch her or something.

"Hey, Harley," Max said awkwardly.

"Max," he said, giving him a quick nod and not meeting his eye. Rose would have cared, but she was too busy trying to breathe. "Come on, Rose. Let's get you checked in."

He put his arm around her waist, tugging at her gently, and for a moment, Rose's hand tightened in Max's pajama T-shirt without her permission. She glanced up at him, his wide, worried eyes, and every part of her wanted him to stay.

"Thanks for bringing me," she croaked, and straightened, heading to the nurse's station under her own steam.

"Good luck," Max said softly. In the reflection of the dark window she saw him raise his hand to wave, then shook his head and ruffled his hair. "See you guys," he said, and sloped off out of the building, his shoulders rounded.

"Okay, how far apart are you?" Harley asked as they were directed toward the waiting room. "It's pretty busy here. One of the midwives said it was the full moon last night, and apparently, it's always busy near a full moon. I guess it's the extra light. Our caveman brains want to be able to see what's going on there…or cavewoman brains, I guess," he said, and chuckled awkwardly.

"Harley, you're rambling."

"Yeah, I know. Oh, I got you a dressing gown." He glanced down at Max's dressing gown. "Well, a spare dressing gown, and some pajamas and some huge granny pants. Also, some granola bars and these pads. Got some real funny looks at the checkout with those. Oh God, here we go."

Rose doubled over, leaning hard against the wall, and Harley dropped the shopping bag and lifted her up into an embrace. "Do that humming thing Crystabel was talking about. Let's walk it off, come on, you can do it."

"Rose Pereira?" called a soft woman's voice.

"Over here," Harley squeaked and cleared his throat. "Sorry, she's just having another contraction."

"Bless," said the midwife sympathetically, stroking Rose on the shoulder. "As soon as you're ready, we've got a room for you. Let's get you comfortable."

CHAPTER TWENTY-EIGHT

Into Battle

There was literally nothing comfortable about any of it. The entire experience seemed endless to Rose. Even the gas and air didn't seem to take the pain away, just made her drift above it, out of control and out of her mind. Voices seemed to echo, and she heard the words long seconds before their meanings crept through into her mind, so that she started to wonder if she'd become able to tell the future. She pulled the mouthpiece away to test out her theory, and the pain was so all-encompassing that she let Harley guide it back, clutching it like her life depended on it.

By the time she was pushing, eighteen hours after her waters had broken, she was so exhausted she could feel her eyes rolling back into her head between every wave. Harley squeezed her hand hard, giving her something to work against, and pulled her lower lip away from her mouth because she bit down on it every single time.

"One more," the midwife shouted, a different midwife to the one who'd welcomed her. She'd been here so damn long, the shifts had changed. "One more," said the doctor, and after the fifth time they tried to encourage her like that, she stopped believing them.

"Trust me," the midwife said, leaning over and holding her gaze, ice blue eyes boring into hers. "One more big push, and your little one will be here, and this'll all be over. You're doing a wonderful thing for Harley here, now look at me. Look at me. You got this."

She pushed, lifting herself off the bed, her body curling in on itself, blood bursting across her tongue as she bit her lip once again. Then there was something huge and painful and wet and hard, and there was a baby on her chest.

Rose stared at it and almost screamed, clutching on to its slimy back. For one crazy, heart stopping moment, she thought it was going to be pulled out of her arms and back inside her, and she clung on tight.

"Oh God. Oh my God, I've got a baby girl," sobbed Harley. "Oh, my baby, my Nina, oh my God." He held his hand over her back, over Rose's hand. "Oh honey, oh, please, may I hold her?"

Rose didn't have the energy to scream *please*, just nodded and slumped back onto the hospital bed, breathing hard, and absolutely certain that she was absolutely never, ever, in a million years, going to do that again.

The baby was grumbling in Harley's arms. She rolled her head to look at them. The doctor had clipped the umbilical cord, and Harley was cradling the baby—Nina, apparently—against his bare chest. The midwife gently draped a blanket against her head and back, and Harley took it with a smile, even as he sniffled, tears dripping off his nose.

"Thank you," he whispered to Rose.

"Hey, no worries," she said sarcastically. "But you can stay away from me with that penis of yours from now on, yeah?"

The midwife, Anna, laughed out loud, throwing her head back. "Well, you're feeling better already, aren't you?"

Rose raised an eyebrow slightly but didn't have the energy to say *no, not really*. Instead, she let herself drift. Around her there were people bustling, and she couldn't bring herself to care what they were doing, whether it was weighing Nina or disposing of the afterbirth or cleaning up. Rose didn't want to know.

She hadn't realised she'd drifted off until Anna gently shook her on the shoulder. "We've got to move you to the ward upstairs until tomorrow, love," she said. "Let's get you in a wheelchair."

"What?" Rose blinked groggily and peered at the clock. "Can't I go home? Melinda was home a couple of hours after."

She smiled. "I'm sorry, love, but not this time of night. There's a lot of admin that needs doing for both you and baby, and the receptionists won't be back until eight tomorrow."

Rose nodded and heaved herself up, staggering into the unwieldy-looking wheelchair. Someone placed Nina into her arms and she looked up in horror. "But...but..."

"I'm sorry," said Harley, biting his lip and very obviously holding back tears. He stroked Nina's eyebrow and fingertips where they poked out of the blanket. "They won't let me take her home yet either, please could you...I know it's a lot to ask. I'm so sorry."

She wanted to scream. But Harley sniffed and wiped his cheeks, still staring, transfixed, at his little girl, and she bit it back. "Yeah, sure. I'll look after her."

He couldn't answer, and when they wheeled her away, she glanced back to see him standing hunched in on himself, both hands pressed over his eyes. One of the other midwives was rubbing his shoulder and offering him a tissue.

Rose turned back to the baby in the crook of her arms and startled when two deep blue eyes looked back at her. "Holy shit, you're awake," she murmured.

The baby grumbled, crinkling up her nose and squirming, rubbing uncoordinated hands across her eyes. "Don't do that, you'll scratch yourself. God, look at those nails of yours. No wonder they sell baby manicure kits."

The nurse or orderly or midwife pushing her—Rose wasn't sure what their job description was—sniggered. "She looks like you," she added, peering over her shoulder as they paused in the lift.

Rose cocked her head to one side. "You think? I think she just looks like a baby, honestly."

The woman chuckled again. "You get used to spotting the differences between different babies when you work here."

"I suppose. This is pretty much the first baby I've ever held."

"Wow. Well, it'll be a learning curve for you, Mum."

"I'm not her mum. I'm her surrogate," she said, and maybe it was the exhaustion, but she didn't feel so coldly humiliated when she said it this time.

The woman smiled and patted her shoulder. "You've made her daddy very happy, I'll bet."

She laughed, and it threatened tears. "Last I saw him, he was sobbing, so we've certainly made him something. Haven't we, Nina?"

Anna was already there to settle her in to a bed on a darkened ward with a smile. "Now, I've explained your situation to the ward sister, and she'll pass it on, okay? But I don't know what you've got planned for feeding Nina, whether you want to try to give her her first meal? Because she's going to start fretting soon. I'm amazed she hasn't already. She's such a placid little thing."

Rose frowned down at her. "I was planning to express and pass the milk on to Harley for a couple of months," she said.

"Well, we can set you up with a pump now and feed her with a bottle, or…"

Rose glanced up at her. "You want me to feed her directly?"

Anna shrugged. "It would be easier for both of you, I'm sure, but I understand you might not want that. We're here for you both, Rose. It's not just about what's best for Nina."

Rose couldn't speak for a moment. Her nose prickled, her throat thickened, and she had to blink rapidly, turning her face away. Anna squeezed her shoulder. "Would you like a hug?" she asked softly.

She was too exhausted to pull her defences back up around her. Her first instinct won out, and she nodded, leaning in to press her forehead to Anna's shoulder as she wrapped her arms around her back, rubbing up and down her spine. "You did brilliantly today," she said in her calm voice as Rose's body shuddered with sobs. "Look at this lovely little human you've brought into the world. You did that, you incubated her and kept her safe for nine months. You've done so well."

A baby in one of the neighbouring beds started crying, a croaky, high pitched wail, and she heard the mother shifting around in the bed to soothe it. Rose straightened, wiping her eyes with both hands.

"Here, lean back carefully. Don't slide on the bed," said Anna.

Rose snorted and used her hands to push herself back carefully. "Yeah, sitting is enough for me." She reclined on the raised head of the bed and looked at Nina, who was starting to fuss a little, shifting her head to the side and opening her little gummy mouth. "I'll try to feed her," she said with a tired shrug. "She's hungry now, isn't she? It'll keep us both awake longer if I don't."

Anna smiled and patted her arm. "Yeah, it will. Thanks, Rose, that'll save us some washing up."

Rose smiled with half her mouth. "I'm going to need a hand with this, though," she said.

"That's what we're here for."

Chapter Twenty-Nine

Long Night

When Rose was done feeding Nina and the midwives settled her into the little transparent plastic cot beside her bed, Rose felt like she'd released a long breath. She sank onto the bed and curled onto her side, aching in every inch of her body and looking forward to sleep.

And then another baby woke up. And when they'd settled, another mum was brought in and settled into a neighbouring bed. And then Nina woke a couple of hours later and needed a nappy change.

Rose felt like screaming, like joining the one baby who couldn't seem to settle down and cried, an exhausted little wail, for nearly an hour. Her eyes itched, and a headache settled in behind her sinuses, and she thought if anyone had dared ask her for anything, she would have thrown things at them.

Eventually, the lights came on in the corridor, and the smell of coffee started drifting in from somewhere. Rose blinked sandy-feeling eyes and hauled herself up to brave the toilet.

Harley arrived the moment the visiting hours started, almost hidden behind a massive bunch of flowers. Rose couldn't help the smile bursting across her face, and watching him tenderly pick up his daughter and cradle her head against his chest when she grumbled made her feel a little bit less exhausted. Or maybe the exhaustion felt a little bit justified.

"How was she last night?" he asked, looking at Rose properly for the first time.

"Better than the baby in the middle bed," Rose said, lowering her voice. "That poor mum burst into tears at about two in the morning, and I think the ward sister took the baby after a while. He wouldn't stop crying. Nina only woke up twice."

The paperwork took hours. Rose learned how to use the breast pump and dozed while Harley walked Nina around, showing her the window, the chair, and all sorts of mundane rubbish. "It's all new to her," he explained, when Rose called him on it. She shrugged and closed her eyes.

Eventually, she found herself dressed in the trackie pants and T-shirt Harley had brought her from Tesco, following him across the car park to his sensible Volvo with its Isofix car seat. He'd set up a little mirror on the headrest of Nina's chair so he could look into his rearview mirror and see her face, which was probably all screwed up right now, considering how much grumbling she was doing. Harley chattered to her the whole way back, reassuring her when she cried, even singing to her at one point. Rose felt like a fly on the wall, watching a happy family.

Harley glanced into the mirror as they pulled up to a red light, and a smile dawned across his face, so soft that Rose almost cried there and then. She wondered if her dad had looked at her like that when he brought her and Mum home from the hospital, if he'd cradled her head in his hand, holding her body close to his chest so she could hear his heartbeat and feel less alone.

Harley pulled up to the pavement outside her flat. "Look at that, perfect parking." He grinned. He hopped out and came around to her door, offering her a hand to help her out. She nearly pushed it away until she tried to engage her core muscles and lift herself from her seat. She grabbed his wrist quickly, and he tucked his hand under her elbow, lifting her gently. "Are you sure you're going to be okay? I can come in and make you some lunch. I know you said you didn't get much rest last night. Nina and I should look after you, shouldn't we, honey?" He waggled his fingers at his little girl through the window.

"Don't be daft, Harley, you need to go bond with your baby." She smirked at him. "Go on, you know you want to cuddle up to her on the sofa and play your entire back catalogue to her. I'll see you tomorrow with more milk, yeah?"

He smiled at her, and before she could react, threw his arms around her, holding her tight. "Thank you so much, Rose. You have no idea what this means to me. I love her so much already," he whispered, his voice thick with tears.

Rose tensed when he grabbed her but relaxed into it, squeezing him back. "You're going to be the best dad in the world, Harley. I can tell." She swallowed hard. "You remind me of my dad."

He pulled back, a huge smile painted over his face, and the resemblance was a bit too much to handle at that point. She thumped him on the arm. "Go on, take your little girl home and give her the grand tour. And try to get some sleep, yeah?"

He nodded. "Call me if you need anything, anything at all, okay? I'll see you tomorrow."

She waved him off, slipped the bag full of her dirty clothes higher on her arm and headed up to her flat.

With nobody watching, nobody expecting anything of her, she felt hollow. Not just physically, her belly floppy and loose and aching where it had once been straining forward and pulling her off balance. She pushed at her door and frowned when it hung open.

"Rose? That you?"

She stepped into her flat. "Max? How did you get in?"

He walked out of the kitchen, drying his hands on a tea towel. His hair was flopping into his eyes, damp with steam from doing the dishes, and the ache inside her grew. "You forgot your keys at my place. I figured you wouldn't mind. Is this okay? Are you okay? How did it go?"

A wave of emotion swelled up in her throat, engulfing her chest, her mind, every pore of her, and she took the three steps forward, pressing herself tight into the curve of his body, burrowing into his comfort, and giving up all pretense at dignity, sobbing unreservedly as he wrapped both arms tight around her, stroking through her hair, kissing her ear, rubbing her shoulder blades and humming soft words that couldn't penetrate through the whirlpool of overwhelmed, exhausted, emotional, pained everything.

Chapter Thirty

Recovery

When Rose emerged from the bedroom, the sky was completely dark. "Did I just sleep for nine hours? In the day?" she croaked.

Max looked up from his phone, his long legs thrown onto the coffee table. "Hey, sleepyhead. Yes, you did."

"God." She yawned. "I'm going to be up all night, aren't I?"

"Probably not," he said. "You just expelled a baby out of your vagina. I reckon you could do with another eight hours or so. Speaking of which, how was it?" He leaned forward to stare at her in morbid fascination.

She grinned. "Like shitting a melon."

"What?" he yelled and threw his head back laughing. "That's the most disgusting thing I've ever heard."

"Accurate, though," she said, raising her eyebrows. "Honestly, it was actually a bit traumatic. God, I sound like an absolute twat saying that. Traumatic."

"No, I can see that," he said, nudging her hip with his toes, much more gently than he usually would. "You were in labour for eighteen hours, then you had to spend the night and got no sleep, and then you gave the baby..." He trailed off. "I'm sorry, are you okay with this?"

She couldn't stand how gently he spoke to her. It made something squirm in a cage inside her chest, howling and screaming to get out. She wanted to fight against it, tell him not to treat her like something so fragile, but there was no energy left for it. "You mean giving the baby up? Yes, I'm fine with it. No, honestly, I am." She looked down and bit her lip.

"You don't sound completely fine with it, you know," he said, shifting closer to run a hand along her shoulders.

"It's not what you think," she said softly. "I really don't feel bad having given Nina to Harley. That's why I did this whole thing, you know? I shouldn't feel bad. But is there something wrong with me? Should I feel awful? Should I miss her like crazy? I mean, I even spent the night with her, shouldn't I have bonded with her, even a little? I breastfed her twice, you know? Just, what's broken in me, as a woman?"

"Nothing," he said fiercely. "You're not broken at all. You are you. All this bullshit about women being naturally maternal, all it does is hurt everyone. Nobody can believe you don't want children. Even you're punishing yourself for being non-maternal. And Harley, nobody can believe that he'd be better for the baby than you, even though he loved Nina since the day he found out she existed."

Rose sniffled and nuzzled closer to him, feeling the bars holding the desperate creature inside her bend a little. "Honestly, if anyone's going to know about the bullshit of gender roles, it's you, huh?"

"Absolutely," he said, kissing her head. "So listen to me, I know stuff."

❖

The next few weeks were strange, almost dreamlike at times. Her centre of gravity was off, she was in the throes of the longest period of her life, bleeding and cramping as her uterus shrank back to its normal size, and the hormones that had flooded her body for nine months were throwing her emotions all over the place as they sought their balance. Max spent most evenings with her. Now the nights were closing in, he wasn't working such long hours and was able to drive up in the early evening, lying on her lap to watch TV. Often, they didn't even talk, snuggling together and not discussing the elephant in the room.

Miho called her the day after she got home, tentatively asking how she was, so obviously tiptoeing around her feelings that Rose snapped at her that she was just in physical pain, not emotional, and if Miho could stop treating her like a grieving mother, that would be great. Miho apologised, and Rose felt like crap. She considered going out, seeing some of her friends or even inviting them over, but the idea of three weeks of seclusion in her flat with only Max to break the silence every now and again was too tempting to resist.

She did see Harley every day, but it was only for a few minutes when he dropped by to pick up her expressed milk. He looked frazzled and exhausted most days but always had a huge smile for her.

Even though she expressed milk diligently, somehow, she still managed to get mastitis, waking up one morning shaking with flu symptoms, stabbing pains radiating out from her nipple. She curled up in her bed and felt horrible until Harley knocked on the door.

He gasped. "Oh my gosh, are you okay?"

She glared at him. "You're not supposed to point out when someone looks like shit."

"No, but you look so poorly, have you got a bug?" She noticed he stepped backward, trying to surreptitiously hold Nina's car seat away from her.

"I'm not contagious, Harley. I've got mastitis. If you touch me, I'm going to have to kill you."

He winced. "Oh, man, I'm sorry." He hesitated. "You know, they said that the best thing for mastitis is to—"

"I tried expressing this morning, and unless you want to hear a grown woman scream, you better keep that little nugget of advice to yourself, yeah?"

"Okay," he said, shutting his mouth quickly.

"I don't think I'm going to be able to get any more for her, mate, sorry."

"No, no, it's fine. She's already had the important immunity stuff, and we always knew we were going to move on to formula. It is what it is, and you didn't have to do all that. I really appreciate it, Rose."

"Don't, Harley," she whined. "You're making me feel like a cow again."

"That really wasn't my intention."

"I know. Look, you're so damn nice, that's how I feel when you're around, okay? Sorry."

"Oh." He ducked his head and bit his lip. "Is that why…"

She pressed her face into her hand. "I don't know," she said softly. "I don't think actually loving anyone has anything to do with stuff like that, though. I think it's the other way round. If I'd loved you, I wouldn't have felt mean when I'm around you, you know? I would have felt right. I guess." She shrugged. "What do I know about love?"

He tilted his head to one side. "I dunno, how does Max make you feel?"

"I'm not in love with Max," she snapped.

He blinked. The moment drew out. Finally, he turned, picking Nina up. "Do you need me to get you anything?"

"Harley…"

"Rose," he said firmly. "It's none of my business."

"I'm sorry." She sighed, closing her eyes in frustration.

"No, no, that's not what I mean." He sighed, rubbing his

head, and set Nina down again. "Look, I don't think what happened between us matters to me anymore. I mean, I got Nina out of it, and that's such a miracle. I could be happy for the rest of my life just knowing she's here, and you made that possible. I think I'll love you forever just for that. No, wait. I'm not finished." He waited until she was looking at him, holding her gaze. "I don't think I'm *in* love with you anymore, though."

She blinked. "Uh, you're not?"

He bit his lip and shook his head. "I don't think so. I mean, I used to think about you. All the time. I used to want you in my arms. I used to want to kiss you and tell you everything and hear your entire life story, and whenever something big happened, I wanted you to know. When you were near me, any moment I wasn't touching you felt wrong. And now, I don't know. Maybe I know that's never going to happen, so I've let it go, or something? Either way, I don't wake up aching for you."

"Harley…"

"And I think you need to really think hard about whether there's anyone in your life you want like that. Someone you cling to even when you think you shouldn't, someone you're comfortable with, someone you want to touch and hold on to and…and love. All the time. I think you need to figure that out. And I'm not saying so to be mean, or I don't know, get some sort of revenge, or whatever you're thinking. I just want you to be happy."

He stood and patted her on the shoulder, walked to the fridge to get the last batch of milk, and let himself out. Rose sat on the sofa and stared into thin air.

When her phone rang, she startled, picking it up with a frown. "Hello?"

"Hello," Max said, drawing out the last sound. "Why do you sound so confused?"

She stood and walked to the window, restless. "I dunno, I didn't mean to. What's up?"

"Just calling to see if you want to watch a movie tonight. It's too wet to do any more discing. The cultivator keeps getting clogged up, so Jamie's sent us home."

Rose clenched her hand into a fist against the windowsill. "Uh, I'm feeling a bit rough, actually."

"Aw," he said, and she could hear the sympathetic frown in his voice. "Want me to get some soup from the shop?"

"No, honestly, I'm going to go to sleep. You should keep away, you know, in case you catch it."

There was quiet on the phone, slight shifting noises. "Yeah, okay," he said, his voice strained. "When do you think—"

"Fucking hell, Max, it's not like I need anyone here," she snapped.

"Yeah, okay," he said, his voice cold. Hurt. "Call me, then, when you're ready to…" He took a deep breath. "No, you know what? Fuck this. Fuck you, Rose. I deserve better than this."

The line went dead. Rose didn't cry.

Chapter Thirty-One

Looking Out

Rose returned to work three weeks after Nina was born. Slipping back into that world was surreal. She kept expecting everyone else to be so different, to have changed so much since she went away, but they were still all doing the same projects, still gossiping about the same stuff. Still buying the same food at lunch. She wondered why it felt so jarring, and a small voice at the back of her mind reminded her that she was the one who'd been on the journey. She was the one far away from them now.

Helen came up to her desk, asking how she was with her jaw clenched and her eyes fixed on some point to the left of her shoulder. Rose shrugged. "Getting back to normal."

She hesitated for a moment as if she was waiting for something, but Rose stayed quiet, awkwardly looking at her, and she drummed her fingers on the top of the shelf of her cubicle. "Great. That's good. Okay. So have you checked on your samples? Any losses during incubation?"

"Not significant ones. They seem to have dealt with the extended period in the nitrogen freezer well enough. Which is pretty much what we expected," she pointed out.

Helen nodded. "Good. Excellent. Fine, well, good to have you back."

Rose gave her the most insincere smile she could muster

and watched her retreat back to her office. Well, at least she was talking to her.

She didn't try very hard to keep up with the other NCT parents, but when Nadine texted her to invite her over to meet baby Alexis, she put on her most social face and bought a box of chocolates before driving over to her village, the weak November sun glinting in her eyes as she swore at the satnav on narrow country lanes.

"Rose! Hi, I'm so glad you could come. Come in, would you like some tea?"

"Oh no, you don't." Rose grinned. "Sit down, and I'll make the tea. I learned that much from our classes."

"You're my hero. My last three cups have gone cold. Come in and meet my little man."

She peered over the edge of the moses basket where a little crumple-faced baby was snoozing, a dummy wiggling in his mouth. "Ah, bless him," she said, trying to inject as much enthusiasm into her voice as possible. "How many days?"

"Four," she said with a sigh, sitting gingerly on a kitchen chair. "I'm utterly exhausted but wouldn't change a minute of it."

Rose busied herself finding cups and teabags and shifting dirty dishes to the dishwasher. "Aw, Rose, you don't have to do that," Nadine said.

"See, your words say that, but your voice says *Rose, I will worship you forever if you make my plates clean.* Sit back and enjoy it."

"I really will worship you forever," she said, affecting a pathetic look.

Rose laughed. "How was the labour?"

"Ugh. God. Thirty-two sodding hours."

"Thirty-two?" Rose squeaked, whirling to gape at her.

Nadine nodded. Her eyes were dark rimmed, her bob lank

and greasy, and Rose was utterly horrified. "I thought eighteen hours were bad enough."

"They are bad enough," she said. "Honestly, the first three hours of contractions were bad enough for me. But Alexis was facing the wrong way up, so the first twenty-four hours or so of contractions were him rolling over."

"What, you mean he was breech?"

"No, nothing so dramatic. He was just lying faceup. Babies should be facedown to come out correctly." She shrugged. "Crystabel mentioned it, but I didn't really take it in either."

"God, Nadine, I'm sorry."

"Don't be." She smiled, the manic gleam of a true believer coming into her eyes. "I got Alexis at the end."

Rose laughed and shrugged. "If you say so."

"Oh, Rose, I'm so sorry, that was so insensitive."

"Huh? Not at all. We all knew I was only having the baby for Harley."

Her eyes softened, and she took the mug from Rose. "Are you sure you won't...you know."

Rose frowned and sat across from her. "What?"

"Well, have you considered...you know."

"No?"

"You and Harley. I mean, now you've met baby Nina—I saw her last week, she's a darling—you must be rethinking things, right?"

"Nadine..."

"I mean, I know you didn't really want to be a mum, but surely now Nina's here, don't you want to try to make things work with Harley? For her?"

Rose looked at her in silence for a moment. She really had been trying to be kinder, more thoughtful, and Nadine had just had a baby four days ago. She forced herself to remember the emotional weirdness of the days after Nina was born, and she'd been getting vast quantities of sleep, which Nadine didn't look like she'd had.

"Look, I know it's hard to believe," she said, and she forced her voice to stay gentle, polite, against all her instincts. "But I really do think this is the best thing I can do for her. She's a lovely little baby, as babies go. But I'm not her mum. I'm not."

Nadine shrugged and looked at her sadly, as if she didn't believe her, as if she could see some tragic future for the three of them, and it made Rose want to scream and throw things. She glanced down at Alexis and did neither of those things. But the conversation was stilted, and when she left, she didn't think she'd be coming back any time soon.

The flat was quiet and cold when she got home, even though the thermostat said it was running at normal temperature. Rose wrapped Mum's old afghan around her shoulders and leaned on the windowsill, staring out at the late autumn drizzle, a cup of tea warming her hands. Something had shifted under her ribs in the last months, and she felt like her mind was in a constant battle with itself, trying to keep things how they were, retreat back to the comfortable fog of before.

She found herself texting Miho, of all people, asking if she wanted to come over for takeaway. She stared at the text after it had sent, watched the little icon turn to *received*, and wondered at herself.

Miho brought wine this time, and Rose almost fell on it. "God, I haven't had alcohol in nearly a year," she whined.

"I know." Miho smiled, amused. "Harley told me you can't breastfeed anymore, so I figured you're safe to drink again. I can't believe you haven't already."

Rose turned away to fetch wineglasses in case Miho somehow read on her face that she didn't actually have anyone else to drink with. Maybe she never had. There was a lump rising in her throat, and she felt the strangest urge to hug Miho. She cleared her throat instead. "I got pizza, hope you're hungry. They had a two for one deal on."

"I'm starving," Miho said, turning to the coffee table. "Want to stick on *Strictly*?"

Rose nodded, bringing plates and wineglasses over, and they crossed their legs, balancing their food on their knees. "Are you back in your old jeans?" Miho asked, eyes wide as she saw the sparkly black jeans Rose had squeezed into that morning.

Rose grinned smugly. "Sure am. Although I have to admit, there's a lot of extra loose skin that's been sort of folded in there."

Miho laughed. "Hey, it still counts. How are you feeling, by the way? I can't believe I haven't seen you since you had Nina."

"I'm good," she said, nodding. "Still on the biggest period of my life. Sorry, a bit TMI."

"Oh my God, really? Like, you've been bleeding since Nina was born? Is that normal?"

"Yeah, things they don't tell you until you get knocked up, huh? Your uterus has to shrink back down to this size"— she made a fist—"and that's a lot of tissue to get rid of."

Miho looked horrified. "Why does nobody ever tell us this stuff?"

"Because if they did, the human race would grind to a halt? Honestly, though, think back to your sex-ed classes. It was all periods and contraception, and that's the last you hear about it. I guess it's less relevant to most people to be learning about the horrors of childbirth and pregnancy at that age, and then after you leave school, when do you have the chance?"

"Suppose so," she said, slumping back on her chair. "But I've never even heard other mums talking about it, not really."

"That's because they're traumatised and want to forget it." She laughed. "Honestly, if I knew I might have to do it all over again to have another child, I'd probably want to blank it all from my mind." She nudged her. "Consider yourself inducted into the inner circle."

Miho widened her eyes, staring down at her pizza like it held the secrets of the universe. "I always thought I wanted children," she said, dazed.

Rose cackled. "Have I converted you?"

She was quiet for a moment, a little frown on her face as she took a bite of pizza. "Nah," she said, settling back and watching some celebrity Rose had never heard of twirling around in a spandex jumpsuit. "I guess it's worth it. I want to be a mum one day. I'm looking forward to all of it, you know? Babies, toddlers, little kids asking why all the time, teenagers being sleepy and intense and emo."

"How can you possibly look forward to raising teenagers?"

She shrugged. "I guess I want to be there for someone. The way I wished someone had been there for me, you know? I want to listen when they tell me they feel like they might be the only person in the world some days. I don't want to flick my hands at them and tell them to stop being so stupid, that they're selfish, spoilt, they don't know how lucky they are. I knew I was lucky. I knew lots of people had it worse off, but I don't know. I guess it didn't stop me feeling sad and alone and misunderstood all the time."

Rose sighed and put her pizza down and looked at Miho's profile as she stared at the TV flashing colours dancing over her pale skin. "Miho, why do you even hang out with me? Honestly? You're so damn nice, and I'm not."

She looked over at her, eyes wide, confused. "I don't

know?" She shrugged. "You know, you're not as horrible as you seem to think you are."

"Yeah, right. Sure."

"No, really, you're not. You're not very thoughtful, that's true. But I think, after Chelsea and I came over and we were talking about things, well, I think you have a good reason for acting the way you do."

Rose shook her head, frowning. "Excuses."

"Well, yes, I suppose. But as soon as you learned you were hurting people, you tried to change how you treat them. You do actually care, as much as you'd like everyone to think that you're this ice queen."

Rose turned back to the TV, her throat aching. "Honestly, I don't know why people would want to put in the effort with me." She laughed. "I mean, there are plenty of people out there who are naturally thoughtful."

Miho shrugged and smiled. "I don't know. You're funny and sassy and strong. You make me laugh." She shrugged again. "I guess I've never had reasons for liking any of my friends. They're my friends, and that's why I like them."

Rose bit her tongue, wishing she could be brave enough to tell Miho she was going to get hurt one day, that someone like Rose was going to take her naivete and use it against her. She felt her hands curl into fists. If that ever happened, Rose would beat the living crap out of the person who hurt Miho.

Chapter Thirty-Two

Cool Aunt Rose

Rose knocked on Harley's door, shifting from foot to foot, fiddling with the teddy under her arm, gnawing on her lower lip, and fighting the urge to run far, far away.

"Rose," said Harley as he opened the door, his face breaking into a wide smile. "Come in. You should have texted to let me know you were coming. I'd have tidied up a bit."

"Why do you think I didn't text, Harley? You shouldn't be tidying on my account. In fact, that's what I'm going to do." She grinned. "I did listen to some of the NCT lessons."

Harley slumped slightly, and she frowned to see his eyes tear up a little. Come to think of it, he looked utterly exhausted, his hair no longer in a smooth arc around his head but lopsided and lying in clumps in one place and flattened on one side. His eyes were red rimmed, and the dark circles under them were so deep, he looked like he'd been punched in the nose. "Harley, is everything okay?"

He nodded, and that smile was most definitely forced. "Yeah, I'm great."

Nina started howling, and Harley jumped. "Oh God," he groaned, his voice cracking. "I'll be right back, just, uh…" He waved his hand in the direction of the kitchen.

"Go do your thing," she urged. "I'll make tea."

"Oh, yeah, but…" He darted a glance up the stairs as Nina's cries reached a new pitch. "Okay, yeah."

She had two cups of steaming tea and was halfway through a load of dishes when she heard steps behind her, and Harley walked in with a tearful Nina chewing on her dummy. "Look who's here," he said, pointing to her. "It's *Rose*, isn't that wonderful? And she's—Oh, Rose, you didn't have to do that."

"Shut up and sit down. I'm making you lunch as well."

His lip wobbled, and to her absolute horror, tears started welling up and spilling over, falling unchecked. He sniffled and tugged Nina closer, closing his eyes as he cried, cuddling his little girl like a comfort blanket. "Sorry," he said. "God, sorry, this is so stupid." He wiped his eyes with his thumb. "It's just that I'm so tired. She's perfect. Nina's the best thing that's ever happened to me, and I wouldn't change her for the world, but she's having so much trouble sleeping, and I think her tummy hurts, and the only way she sleeps is in bed with me. She lies on my chest, and it's safe, honestly." He chuckled. "I don't seem to move at night anymore. I wake up every morning with my arms up over her back, in exactly the same position I fell asleep. I usually have terrible dead-arm, but it's so lovely. She's so beautiful when she's asleep, but my God, she doesn't sleep nearly enough."

"Look, why don't you go and sleep for a bit now?"

He looked around, all the excuses and protests forming on his reluctant tongue.

"Go on, you know you need it," she pushed. "I'll wake you when lunch is ready, okay?"

"Are you sure?"

"Absolutely. You said she sleeps best on your chest, so go do that now, both of you need a bit of a nap."

"I shouldn't really mess up her routine."

"Sod the routine. She doesn't know her schedule, she's two months old. Go on, sleep."

A shy smile broke over his face, and he hugged Nina a little tighter, smiling up at her with those old worshipful eyes that always made her so uncomfortable and unworthy. "Thanks, Rose."

"Go on, time's a-wasting."

When Harley and Nina had headed off upstairs, Rose let out a long breath and finished the washing up. The fridge was woefully understocked, and she frowned, wondering where the hell the others from Stare at the Sun were when Harley needed them. But then she remembered it wasn't like she'd been there for him either, so it probably wasn't her place to judge. Instead, she jumped back in the car and went on an Aldi run.

They were both still sleeping when she got back nearly forty-five minutes later, and she smirked to herself as she made a huge batch of soup and filled the slow cooker up with pork belly and pearl barley, dumping in ginger, allspice and garlic, chopping aubergines, and covering them all with tinned tomato and stock. He'd only have to chuck a bit of rice into a saucepan and he'd have enough curry to see him through for almost a week.

The doorbell went as she was cleaning up the mess, and she opened the door, the dishcloth slung over one shoulder. "Hi, can I help you?"

"Oh, hello," said the middle-aged white woman at the doorstep. "I'm the health visitor."

"The what now?"

The lady blinked at her. "The health visitor. This is Nina Henderson's house, isn't it?"

"Oh, yeah, come on in, I'll go and get them. Uh, go into the kitchen, I guess." She ran up the stairs to Harley's room, tapping softly on the door. "Harley," she whispered. "There's a health visitor here."

Harley shifted and mumbled, one hand still firmly on Nina's back, the other rubbing his eyes. "Huh?"

"Health visitor. Should I tell her to bugger off?"

"Health v—oh, God, I'd forgotten. Shit." He struggled to rise, still holding Nina carefully, cradling her head so she barely even noticed the shift. "God, I can't believe I slept through her knocking."

"Hey, you were tired. You needed it. Come on, then, I'll get the kettle on."

"Thanks, Rose," he mumbled, still not entirely awake. He followed her downstairs slowly, yawning.

Rose flashed an insincere smile to the health visitor. "Would you like some tea?" she asked.

"That would be lovely. Milk, no sugar, please. Are you Nina's mum?"

"Uh…" She glanced over at Harley.

"Hi, Sarah," he said, still looking sleepy. "Sorry, yes, this is Rose. She's Nina's birth mother."

"What a pleasure to meet you at last," she said, holding out her hand. Rose shook it with a brusque nod. "It's good to have you here as well. I'm sure you want to know how Nina's progressing."

Rose shrugged but bit back her honesty.

"Have you got Nina's red book?" Sarah was still looking at Rose, who felt like a rabbit in the headlights.

"Uh, I have," said Harley, waving it in the air.

"Oh, thanks, Harley. What a good dad he is." She chuckled conspiratorially to Rose.

"Yeah, he's pretty awesome," she said because that kind of honesty was probably socially acceptable.

"Right, now, if you'll all come into the sitting room, we can get Miss Nina weighed again. How's she been this week, Rose?"

Rose bit her tongue. "I have no idea," she said, trying very hard to be polite. Sarah cocked her head and frowned in confusion. "I'm sorry, do you not understand what our situation is?" Rose asked, trying very hard to control her irritation.

"Oh, well, Harley told me you weren't together, but I figure since you're here—"

"I did explain you were the surrogate," Harley said softly, looking at Rose out of those big sad puppy eyes. She felt the familiar irritation rise at that look but strangely realised it wasn't because of him.

"I really think you should be talking to Harley," she said stiffly. "I'm only visiting."

"Oh, of course. I see how it is." She smiled. Rose raised an eyebrow and refrained, heroically, from saying, *I really think you don't.* She even managed to restrict her eye roll until she got back into the kitchen. Behind her, she could hear the woman interrogate Harley and even wake Nina up just to strip her bare and weigh her. Nina wailed, and Harley spoke sympathetically to her, and Rose gritted her teeth.

By the time she brought the tea in, Harley was rocking Nina and singing to her, one of his own songs. "Thank you, Rose," said Sarah, taking the mug and sipping it before placing it down on the floor by the sofa. "Now, is there anything else you wanted to ask? Is she feeding well, sleeping well?"

"She's been a bit unsettled recently," Harley admitted. "Her sleep was excellent until about a week ago, and then she started getting really fretful in her moses basket. I'd settle her and put her to bed asleep, and she'd wake up within minutes. I've tried warming the blankets up with a hot water bottle before she goes down, I've tried—"

"Are you making sure you remove the hot water bottle before you put her in?" Sarah interrupted sharply.

"Yes, of course," he said, blinking. "Um, what else. I've

tried burping her a little longer and staying next to her with my hand on her tummy, but really, the only time she gets any real sleep is when she's lying on me."

"Oh, but you're not falling asleep yourself, are you?" she said.

"Well, I'm trying not to, but really, I've tried everything else, and when she sleeps on my chest, she gets a full five hours, which is heavenly, and it's helping me so much more—"

Sarah was shaking her head, her lips pursed like she'd sucked a lemon. "No, no, no, that won't do. You really must try harder. Co-sleeping comes with a dramatically increased risk of cot-death, and if you are as tired as you say you are, that's going to make it much more likely that you'll roll over on her in your sleep and crush her. And further down the line, especially if you're…" She glanced at Rose. "Rekindling your romantic life, then you're going to cause more trouble for yourself. I really must insist that you stop co-sleeping immediately."

"For the last time, we're not rekindling our romance," Rose snapped.

"I'm terribly sorry," she said, nodding over to her. "I misunderstood. But either way, it's not appropriate. And in that case even more so, for a single father co-sleeping with a daughter."

Harley looked down, and Rose gritted her teeth as his eyes started filling with tears again. She stood. "Right, that's it," she said. "You're leaving."

Both of them snapped their gaze to her, shocked.

"No, really," she said. "You come in here with your assumptions and your little party line, you ignore Harley in favour of the only other woman in the room because you figure a uterus makes me much more likely to understand Nina's needs, even though Harley's been her sole carer since she was less than twelve hours old, and now you're upsetting him by implying...well, what are you implying? That because he's a single father that it's somehow *dodgy* for him to share a bed with his daughter? Are you fucking kidding me?"

Sarah gaped, opening and shutting her mouth.

"No, I don't want to hear anything you have to say," Rose snapped, holding up her hand. "Within the last five minutes you've implied Harley will either put his romantic life above his daughter's wellbeing, and that he's some sort of paedophile in the making just because he's male and single? Have you actually met Harley? Have you seen how he cares for Nina?" She shook her head, a disgusted sneer forming. "I'm going to be lodging a formal complaint with the Oxfordshire health centres and requesting a new key worker for him because you are going to cause him to have an anxiety attack and spiral into depression, and then you'll be happy and vindicated because your assumptions about single black fathers or whatever will have come true."

She practically chased the woman out the door and kicked it shut, standing for a moment to glare at the wood until she'd calmed down a bit. She took a deep breath and turned around.

Harley was standing at the doorway to the kitchen. "A formal complaint, huh?" he said softly.

"Damn right, a formal complaint." She snorted, marching past him. "That sanctimonious bat. What does she know about Nina? How does she even expect you to get any sleep when you've tried everything? Didn't she listen? Ugh. I can't even with her."

Harley chuckled, and she turned to glare at him. He had his mouth pressed in a kiss to Nina's temple as she squirmed and sucked on her fist, staring out at the bright light coming through the kitchen window. "You really think she was wrong? I mean, she ought to know, right? She's a health visitor."

Rose let out a long breath and sagged against the counter. "I don't know about the numbers," she admitted. "God knows I haven't exactly done my research. And maybe I'm biased, having slept between my parents for years as a very little kid, but the way she spoke to you? That wasn't acceptable. You can't let people like her push you around, you know? You're such a gentle, passive guy, but you're a dad now. You've got to be Nina's hero. You've got to stand up for the two of you, yeah? Because there's going to be people all over the place who look at you and see numbers before they see you. You've got to push first."

He sat at the table and lowered Nina into a little bouncy chair, clipping a mobile over the top of her. Nina started batting at the plastic rattly zebra, and he smiled at her fondly for a moment. "I do know that," he said. "I'm not really that naive, you know."

"Could have fooled me," she said, raising an eyebrow.

"You know, you think I'm a pushover," he said. "But I talked you into nine months of, in your words, infection with a human parasite, followed by eighteen hours of labour and a recovery that's probably still taking place." He raised his eyebrows, still smiling kindly, but she could see that steel lying under the softness that she'd been so surprised with before. "I do fight. But only when it matters."

She pinched her lips together. "Eat your soup, Gandhi."

He grinned, tied his afro back with a wide band, and took the bowl and spoon from her. "Thank you, Rose. For everything."

"You're welcome. You really are a fantastic dad, you know? But I think it would be best if you don't introduce me as the birth mother anymore. Maybe I could be cool Aunt Rose, how about that?"

His smile was blinding. "You want to be Aunt Rose? I

didn't know if you'd want to be involved at all, but I'd love that. You'll be the best cool aunt ever."

"Look, don't get all excited on me. I don't want to be babysitting every weekend or anything."

"I know," he said, smiling down at his soup. "But still. Aunt Rose. It suits you."

She rolled her eyes and ate her soup.

"How's Max?" he asked, looking up, completely innocent.

"Ha ha," she mumbled. He frowned at her. "Oh, come on," she said. "Like you don't know."

"I've been at home with Nina for two months, Rose. I know literally nothing. Nothing. I'm so sleep deprived, my brain has seeped out of my ears and made a mess of my pillow."

She laughed so loud Nina startled. "Sorry, kiddo." She giggled. "Your daddy has a way with words." She looked into her bowl, and her smile faded. "I haven't seen Max for weeks."

Harley put his spoon down. "What?" he said sharply. "Oh, Rose, what now?"

"Why are you assuming it's my fault?"

"I'm assuming you've pushed him away again. I'm assuming you realised you were falling in love with him and ran the hell away because that's what you do, you idiot. Rose!"

"Hey," she spluttered, her face flushing bright red. "Wind your neck in."

"No. No, I will not, because you literally just told me to fight when things are important, and this is important. What are you doing, Rose? Why do you insist on pushing people away any time they might actually mean something to you? I've seen the way you look at him. I saw the way you hung on to him at the hospital, and you've never looked at me that way."

He looked at his food, his forehead creasing. "And if I'm honest, I saw the way you looked at him before we got together, too. I hoped…" He shook his head. "It doesn't matter now. What matters is you actually not sabotaging the one relationship in your life that might actually mean something to you."

"I don't need anyone," she snapped back, her heart beating fast and painful, her chest aching, the words hard to push out past the treacherous lump in her throat that came out any time she thought too hard about Max. "I don't need anyone. I'm fine by myself."

"And so you should be," he retorted, his eyes alight with ferocity. "You don't love someone because you need someone, that's a codependent mess. You love someone because you choose them."

She blinked at him, mouth opening and closing, and thought of Max's fingers carding through her hair in her bedroom, talking about the act of love being a choice.

"Oh, Rose, I'm sorry," Harley said softly. "I never meant to make you cry."

She put her hands up to her cheeks and was dully surprised when they came away wet. "I don't want to need anyone," she whispered.

"I know," he said, coming around the table to wrap his arms around her. She fought for a moment, then leaned against his chest, tears soaking into his soft T-shirt. "I know."

CHAPTER THIRTY-THREE

Serenity

It felt raw to know herself, to walk through town as the wind howled around her ankles sending what felt like shards of ice under her skin and know that she'd screwed everything up so comprehensively that she might not be able to fix it.

She stopped in front of a window display, the glass glittering with Christmas lights, and stared at her own reflection. Forced herself to hold her own gaze rather than flickering over the next thing she needed to do, whether she needed to stand straighter, whether her makeup was still right.

It felt like the world held its breath. Like there was the distinct possibility that she'd shatter with the acceptance she was building up to.

"Rose?"

Rose startled violently and snapped her head around. "Serenity, hi. What are you doing here?"

Serenity, her tiny frame draped with brown shawls and blankets, a sling strapping her baby to her front, gestured to the shop Rose had been staring at. "Some last-minute shopping."

"Oh yeah," Rose said, looking properly at the gifts in the window. "Christmas."

"Yule, actually," she said with a smile. "Crunchy granola mum, remember? I'm pagan."

"Huh," said Rose, raising an eyebrow. "I have no idea what that means."

"It means we celebrate most holidays by getting together over good alcohol and seasonal food and dance naked around fires."

Rose gave her a flat look until Serenity laughed. "Okay, fine, not that last bit. Unless it's Beltane." She winked. "Would you like to go and get a cup of tea? Little Mary's got a blue nose, haven't you, darling?" She bopped the baby on the nose.

"Sure," Rose sighed. "Want me to carry anything?"

Going for a warm drink with Serenity and a baby was like an explosion had hit Costa Coffee. Serenity shed layer after layer of what looked to Rose like curtains, eventually exposing Mary: first a shock of black hair, then a wildly flailing arm, then a round face with wide blue eyes. She peeled her out of the sling and propped her on her knee, turning her outward and somehow managing to keep her from grabbing the pot of tea.

"That's better," she said as if the entire performance hadn't spread their stuff over half the café. The baristas didn't seem to mind, smiling and waving at Mary every time they had to clear a table nearby. "How have you been, Rose?" Serenity asked.

"Uh," Rose said.

Serenity put her head on one side. "That bad, huh?"

"No. No, it's fine. I'm fine," she said, and dredged up a smile. It felt like a disappointment. She took a deep breath. "It's…"

Serenity smiled at her. "You don't have to tell me, Rose,

we're not best friends. Even if we were, you wouldn't have to tell me anything."

Rose frowned at her latte. "How's life with a baby around the house?" she asked instead.

"Loud," said Serenity. "Smelly. Strangely entertaining. I'm lucky, the community I live in is very open. People are always in and out of each other's houses. I get plenty of rest. Someone's always offering to take the baby to give me a chance to rest. I've done it myself for other mothers, and I'll do it again in the future."

"Wow, that wouldn't suit me at all," Rose said, shaking her head. "I like my privacy."

"Yes, I suppose that is the trade-off. You know, I always thought it was impossible for anyone to not want the kind of life I live, but I think I hadn't met enough people. You and Nadine would be miserable there."

Rose blinked. "Really? You're not going to try to convince me?"

"No," she said thoughtfully. "And I'm starting to realise that you really have made the right decision about baby Nina. Some people don't want babies. I don't have to understand it to accept it."

"Um, yeah, that's…" Rose frowned and prodded at her latte foam with her spoon. "And you're okay with that?"

"It's not really about me, is it?"

"No, I mean, you're okay with changing your mind? Like, you and Nadine had pretty firm beliefs, I think. Nadine still thinks I'm going to regret it and want Nina back. I was sort of expecting you to be the same."

Serenity sat back and moved Mary on her lap, handing her a teether shaped like a little bee. "I think it's important to stick to your beliefs, sure. But it's okay to change them when you get new information."

Rose bit her lip and stared into her drink. "I think I really like Max," she blurted.

Serenity blinked at her. Rose laughed, almost breathless, giddy. "I really like him," she said. "I don't want to pretend that I'm all heartless anymore. I don't..." She gulped. "I really like him."

"Oh, dear," said Serenity, leaning forward and handing her a tissue as she hunched her shoulders and cried. "Oh, Rose. Isn't that a good thing? To know you're capable of feeling that way?"

Rose nodded. "But I've properly screwed it up. I pushed him away again and again, and I was such a cow to him, and I've just...I think that was the straw that broke the camel's back, you know? He was so patient with me, and I think he really liked me, too, and I was such an idiot, and I've blown it completely."

Serenity shifted Mary onto her hip and moved into the seat closer to Rose, wrapping her in a patchouli-scented, one-armed hug. "Come on, now, nothing's ever as hopeless as we think it is."

"God, I'm sorry." She sniffed, sitting up and wiping her face. "I'm causing a scene."

"Someone's got to," said Serenity. "Look at all these people with their boring days. They need some entertainment in their life."

Rose snorted into her tissue, and Serenity looked proud of herself. She still had her arm leant on the back of Rose's chair, and Rose didn't *need* her comfort. She smiled at her anyway and leant on her shoulder. Serenity looped her arm around her and patted her back, and it was...nice. To connect with a person. To be known.

"His friend tried to warn me," Rose said softly. "He kept saying I was being unfair calling us fuck buddies. Oh, sorry."

She put her hand over her mouth and looked at Mary. Mary looked at her toes with the kind of focus Rose only wished she could achieve at work.

"Really, Rose, she's three months old. She can't pick up swear words yet. Carry on."

"Well, I thought, you know, we're adults, we can have no-strings sex, and it'll be fine. Not like my last relationship was a good idea."

She laughed. "Maybe at times. But if you hadn't made the choices you did, Harley wouldn't have Nina."

Rose smiled, then sighed, still leaning on Serenity's shoulder. Mary looked up at her with her wobbly head, and Rose offered her a finger to grab. "I don't think he's going to come back to me this time. He'd be a fool if he did, honestly."

Serenity sighed. "Well, you know what they say about insanity."

"No, what?" Rose sat up and picked her mug up, finishing the cooling coffee.

"The definition of insanity? Doing the same thing and expecting different results."

Rose wrinkled her nose up. "Yeah." She felt her heart sit heavy and cold in her chest. "It really would be insanity to try again, I guess."

"That's not what it means, necessarily. It means you have to try something different. You know, like with Mary. She doesn't seem to feed well in the normal position you see in pictures and everything. She couldn't latch on. But that doesn't mean I had to stop breastfeeding, just that I had to stop trying to force her to feed that way. Now she sits on my knee, and I lean back, and she latches on perfectly."

Rose tapped her fingernail on the mug. "So...I have to try something different?"

Serenity shrugged. "Who knows? I don't know what you

guys keep doing that doesn't work. But if you've realised you have real feelings for him, then that's already something different."

Chapter Thirty-Four

Want and Need

Rose picked her way through the frosty grass and shifted the heavy boom box over her shoulder. She concentrated on how irritating it would be if she'd bought the bloody retro thing for no reason at all rather than allowing her mind to settle on the utter terror of what she'd bought it for.

She looked up, squinting into the low sun, nodded to herself, and shifted the boom box around so she could reach the controls. She plugged her iPod in, swirled through the menu to the playlist and breathed, slow and deliberate. She made sure the volume was up as high as she could stand, placed the boom box on the low patio wall, and pressed play.

The funky saxophone and the heavy, sexy drums blasted through the chilly December morning. Rose bit her lip as Otis Rush's powerful voice started singing "All Your Love." She stood up straight, hands deep in her pockets, and stared at Max's window, trying to keep her mind blank.

There's no one there, she thought, her heart beating fast, cold dread through her body. She was going to stand in Max and Jamie's garden like an idiot until the playlist ran through, and she'd have to put her stupid new machine back in the car and drive home in humiliation. She'd never have the guts to do this again.

Or worse, he was up there. He'd seen who it was, and

he'd developed a sense of emotional self-preservation in the last few weeks, and he was sitting in his room, waiting for her to get the hint and go away. Her stomach felt like lead at the thought. It would only be what she deserved. She couldn't believe she'd done something so stupid, invaded their privacy. She was being as thoughtless and selfish as ever.

She was about to turn off the music and leave when Max's window cracked open, and he leaned out, tousle-headed and blinking sleepily. "Rose? What are you doing?" he croaked.

The thing she'd kept in a cage in her chest for God knew how long warmed and swelled as she saw him, and she tried very hard to hold the smile under control. She ducked her head. "I'm trying to be romantic."

Max was silent, and she looked back up. The music lulled, then flowed into "Purple Rain." "You're being romantic?" Max said, and she couldn't work out the look on his face.

She nodded. "Yeah. Well. I'm not very good at it, as you can see. I mean, according to all the movies and stuff I should be singing but…"

Max nodded. "Prince doesn't deserve that kind of treatment."

She laughed, loud with relief and anxiety. "He certainly does not. And neither do you. My voice is not romantic at all." She bit her lip and tucked her hair behind her ear. "But, well, I was wondering if you'd give me another chance. Not as what we were before but as more."

Max took a deep breath. "You're gonna have to explain a little bit."

"I want to take you out on dates," she said. "Every now and then, you know. Let's not go crazy, I'm still a hermit who doesn't like most people. But most of all, I want to chill on the sofa with you and kiss you and lie on your lap and bring you picnic lunches in the field and not lie about what this is anymore. Not to other people or myself."

She could see Max swallow hard, and she closed her eyes tight, clenching her fists in her pockets because if he told her he wanted nothing more to do with her, it would probably be the most sensible thing he'd done since he'd met her.

"I thought you didn't need anyone," he said roughly.

"I don't," she said, taking her hands out of her pockets and spreading them wide, forcing her cages to break for him. "I still don't *need* you, Max. I can function on a daily basis with nobody around. But I *want* you. I wake up every morning, and I think how much better my world would be with you in it. How much better it was whenever I had to untangle myself from you before work or when you kissed me before you left early in the morning, and you thought I was still asleep."

She used both hands to brush the hair from her face, wanting to pull, cause pain to herself to distract from this feeling of cracking open a shell, exposing her soft underbelly to anyone, but if anyone could be trusted to see her, it was him. She didn't want anyone else to know every part of her. "I know I've tried to push everyone away for years. I thought it would keep me safe. But you managed to get past all my defences, and I hate…I hate that I've hurt you so badly trying to push you out. I care for you, Max, and I never, ever thought I'd care for anyone, not like this. I never wanted to."

She bit her tongue and fell silent. There was another word that wanted to come out, not *care* but another, infinitely more terrifying four-letter word, and she wanted to howl it, complete the destruction of all her boundaries, but it wouldn't be fair to him. If he didn't want her, if he'd pulled back further than she could repair, then it wasn't fair to tell him that.

"You know…I thought that was the closest I'd ever get to

a real relationship," he said, almost too quietly for her to hear. "I thought that was all I deserved."

She shook her head. "You deserve so much more than that shit I put you through, Max, I'm so sorry."

"I know that now," he said, lifting his head and looking at her. "I have a lot of internalised shame and insecurity and bullshit to work through myself, you know."

She nodded and hung her head and wondered if she could hold off on crying until she'd at least gotten back to the car.

"I don't need you, either, Rose," he said. "But...I do want you, still."

She looked up, startled, eyes wide and not believing what she was hearing.

He laughed and wiped his face. "You want to take me out on dates?"

She nodded and cleared her throat. "Candlelit dinners and making out in the back of the cinema and everything."

He laughed again. "God, yeah. Okay. Sure."

She laughed as well, biting her lip and trying to resist jumping up and down.

"Is that Linkin Park playing?" he asked, pointing at the boom box.

"Yeah, 'In Between.'"

"Didn't take you for a fan." He grinned.

She shrugged. "I'm not, but you're into that genre as well, aren't you? I wanted to find a Within Temptation song, like that one you were playing on your phone when we got together, but none of them were quite right."

"You listened to metal for me?"

"I didn't know that's what they were," she mused, looking at the iPod like it was going to tell her.

"Sort of, some of it anyway. Did you make me a playlist and everything?" he teased.

"Yeah. Is that romantic?"

"Dead romantic."

Another window creaked open, and Jamie leaned out. "If you two have sorted your shit out, can you please close the bloody window? You're heating the whole of the bloody Cotswolds."

"Hey, Jamie," Rose yelled. "Max is my boyfriend."

Jamie rolled his eyes. "You finally figured it out. Well done, genius. Now get in here and snog, for God's sake."

Rose almost cracked her face grinning at Max, whose returning smile was just as blinding. "My pleasure."

CHAPTER THIRTY-FIVE

Quiet

Rose lay on Max's shoulder as he stared out the window at the winter rain. She focused instead on the soft grey T-shirt under her fingers, stroking the junction of the material and his collarbone, allowing herself to touch him, not for sex, just for intimacy. He trailed his fingers through her hair absentmindedly.

"I'm sorry," she whispered. "I fucked this all right up."

"No, you didn't," he said. "Look where we are now."

"We could've been here months ago if it wasn't for me trying to be the ice queen."

"We couldn't have," he said. "Look, it's not like you were doing it on purpose, right? You weren't ready to stop being the ice queen, and I wouldn't have believed it was real anyway."

Rose shifted so her head was on the pillow and frowned slightly. "Why not?"

He bit his lip and rolled onto his side to face her. "I'm proud of who I am, you know? I'm proud of what I've been through...but it comes with baggage. It's hard to believe, sometimes, that anyone would want to deal with that."

Rose linked her fingers with his and kissed them, waiting. "It can be easy to be grateful for what you get," he said. "Even if it's only a fraction of what you want. Even if it hurts because it's lacking the really important part. And especially because you've been told you're a freak, and there's something wrong with you. Sometimes, I fall into the trap of thinking I'm lucky I can get a girl to look at me at all, let alone the girl I'm actually..." He took a deep breath. "Actually kind of a little bit in love with."

Rose inhaled sharply. Max's shoulder hunched, and he looked down at the sheets between them, his mouth a thin line and a little frown forming between his eyebrows. "Max," Rose said softly. "Max...I really...shit, I really like you."

It was like a solid rock in her throat, the fear. When had she last said the words? When had she thought them about anyone? Her parents, almost certainly. The first time a boy had said he loved her, she'd done a Han Solo. She'd thought she was being funny. She'd only hurt someone again. That's what Rose Pereira did, she hurt people.

She clenched her hand into a fist and jumped off the cliff. "Max," she said, and kissed him on the cheek, the lips, the forehead. "I love you, too."

Max looked up, then, his face breaking into a wide, involuntary smile. "Damn, Rose, you look like you're facing a firing squad."

"Shut up, you have no idea how terrifying that was." She laughed as the adrenaline fizzled out.

He pushed her over onto her back and kissed her. "Sure I do," he said. His face became serious again, and he looked down at her, strands of black hair falling from behind his ear and casting shadows across his face. "Rose, this is a massive risk for me. You've already broken my heart. Don't act like you're the only one being brave here."

She reached up and caressed his cheek, running her thumb along the soft skin under his eye. "Yeah, okay," she said. "I'm sorry. I'm trying to do better."

"I know." He smiled. "I can tell." He bent and kissed her,

and she held his face, leaning into the sweetness of it without trying to hold herself back. She was still falling, clouds rushing past in exhilarating bursts of colour and cold, but it felt like maybe it would get easier to jump each time.

"Can you tell me if there's anything I should avoid? I hurt you before. I don't want to do it again."

"We're going to hurt each other," he said, resting his weight on her and nuzzling her neck. "We're both going to screw up and be idiots sometimes, Rose. It's not all going to be sunshine and ponies because we've said we love each other."

She tugged his hair and smirked. "Nah, it'll be sunshine and ponies because you're a farmer."

"More like mud and cow poo," he said with a grin. He leaned up on his elbows again. "Okay, here's one thing. The shirt stays on. Don't try to get it off. You can't fix my dysphoria with, like, body worship or whatever."

She narrowed her eyes. "Sure, but if you start wearing your binder too long, I'll be on your case like Jamie. I've actually done my research."

He rolled his eyes. "We've created a monster. Fine. What about you?"

"What do you mean?"

"Is there anything I should avoid? So I don't hurt you?"

She blinked at him, and he frowned. "You know this goes both ways, right? We both have the power to hurt each other. Let's make it less likely, all right?"

"Huh. Yeah, I guess." She stared at the ceiling for a moment. "I guess sometimes, I don't like people. I need to be grumpy and alone, and don't make me feel bad for that, okay? I'll try and tell you when I need space, and I'm really trying not to be catty, but sometimes, it feels like if there's another person near me, I'll scream. And you're one of the only people I can tolerate in those situations, but that might change, and

I wanted you to know, it's not about you. You don't have to make me feel happier. I'll come back. I just sometimes need space to be a grump."

He smiled and ran his fingertip down her nose and over her lips. "Okay," he said. "Yeah. I think this is going to work."

Chapter Thirty-Six

Epilogue

Rose straightened her spine and knocked on the door. Then she gritted her teeth and linked her fingers with Max. She glanced at him out of the corner of her eye, and the smile he was trying to bite away made any potential humiliation worth it.

Harley opened the door with Nina leaning over his shoulder chomping on her fists and making some sort of loud hooting noise. "Hey, guys. Thanks for coming over. Come on in. Max, it's great to see you. It's been ages."

"Hey, Harley," said Max, waving awkwardly, then burying his fingers in his hair.

"Come meet Nina," said Harley, completely ignoring the fact that his ex and his friend were holding hands. Not like Rose had really expected anything different, but well, there had been enough surprise drama. She'd been ready to handle all sorts of reactions ranging from Harley deciding he didn't want Rose to be happy with someone else, to squealing like an excited piglet and clapping his hands when he saw she'd taken his advice.

Being completely ignored in favour of a baby was refreshing, actually. Rose patted Max's hip so he shifted over and pushed past to get to the kitchen, putting a load of frozen food into Harley's freezer and stocking up his cupboard with soup tins.

"Oh, Rose, you didn't have to do that," he called, bustling in.

Rose turned, ready to ask who the hell else was going to, and stopped, openmouthed, when she saw that Max was holding Nina.

He looked desperately uncomfortable, his gangly form hunched around Nina's wobbly body, long fingers patting her back, and a slight frown between his eyebrows as he tried to pull back to see what she was doing and where exactly all that drool was coming from. Rose raised her eyebrows and tried not to smile too obviously. "Having fun there?"

Max narrowed his eyes. "You promised me tea."

"Oh, I'll make that."

"No, you don't, Harley," Rose said, planting a hand in the centre of his chest. "You and Max go and sit down and talk about…I dunno, babies or music or something. Or even better, why don't you have a nap?"

He smiled fondly at her. "I'm fine, Rose. She's sleeping much better now, which means I'm finally getting more than two or three hours a night as well."

"God, I should hope so." Rose groaned, horrified at the thought of such sleep deprivation. "That's against the Geneva convention, you know." She poked Nina's little nose. "Torturer."

"Rose," Harley squeaked, but he was smiling under his reproachful look. He cupped Nina's head in one hand and smiled at her like she was the centre of everything good in the world.

"I have to thank you, actually," he said, glancing back at Rose. "The new health visitor came over the other day, and she is a million times nicer. She's a total hippy. She was telling me about this retreat in India she used to work in, and all the places she's been. She actually reminds me of Crystabel a lot. I know you never really liked her, but she's kind. And she supports my co-sleeping. Off the record, of course. She said there's only so long you can stick to the party line. Sometimes with babies, whatever works is the best you can do."

"Wow, common sense in the NHS. Will wonders never cease?" Max snarked.

"That's great news, Harley," Rose said, thumping him on the arm. He smiled so hard, his eyes almost disappeared. "So when are you back onstage, then? What's the plan?"

He sighed. "Well, officially, I'm going back in February. There's not much in the way of gigs in the winter anyway, so that's lucky. I've got to look into nurseries and stuff. It feels so awful, thinking of putting her in some institution so early. She's so young. Honestly, I'm thinking of packing it in for her, you know?"

"What?" Rose and Max both said at once, horrified. "Harley, no, you can't. You've worked so hard for this."

"She's worth it, though," he said, stroking her cheek as she bobbed her head around, looking over Max's shoulder.

"Oh, come on, Harley," Rose said, slapping his shoulder with the back of her hand. "Don't be ridiculous. You can't assume that you have to give up everything because you've had a baby. You've got to have a life yourself. You've got to raise Nina to see that her dad's not just her dad but his own person with his own dreams, you've got to teach her that if she works bloody hard, she can achieve anything, and the only way to do that is to show her. You don't like nurseries? Well, get a nanny. It's not like you'll need them all the time, and a nanny or an au pair would be more flexible."

He bit his lip. "Yeah, but what about the tour?"

"Take her with you. Take the nanny and the baby, drive

around the country, and okay, you probably won't want to sleep in a tent with a tiny baby, but you could get a camper van or something, you know? Or even stay in a B&B. If you do the numbers, you'll probably find that it'll be cheaper than booking her into nursery."

"But what kind of life is that for a little baby? Or for a child, as she gets older? Assuming we're still doing that in years to come."

"Are you kidding?" Max burst out. "It's an amazing life. Think of how awesome that would have been when you were a kid. You'd have loved it, wouldn't you?"

"And anyway," Rose added. "How else are you going to earn money? If you go back to full-time work doing…what was it you used to do anyway?"

He frowned as if slightly offended. "I worked in a bank. I've told you that."

"And I'm not surprised I forgot, Harley. That's so desperately boring, I've already forgotten again. But if you went back to working in a bank full-time, you'd definitely have to put her into nursery. Probably for much longer hours as well."

He looked at her again. "You don't think that's too, I don't know, greedy?"

"Who says you have to give everything up as soon as you have a baby?" Max said, leaning back to look at him. "You don't have to sacrifice things for the sake of it to prove you're putting her first."

"And maybe it won't work out." Rose shrugged. "If that's the case, you rethink, but you can't assume you've got to give up all your dreams now you're a dad. What kind of message will that send her when she's growing up?"

He pursed his lips and nodded. "I never thought of it like that."

She smiled smugly and patted his shoulder. "You're not nearly as awesome as I am."

He rolled his eyes and went back to chewing his lip and petting Nina, deep in thought. "It might work, you know," he said. "I introduced her to the band a little while ago. They all fell in love with her, obviously. I think they'd be understanding."

"Even Frank?" Rose raised an eyebrow.

"Yeah, even Frank," he said with a sympathetic glance. Then he grinned. "Eliza said she could feel her ovaries weeping, though, which made her new boyfriend look kinda worried."

Rose laughed. "I'm glad it's working out for you, Harley. You deserve it."

"Thanks," he said softly.

"Now, come on, get your arse out of here and go practice. Leave your pride and joy to our tender mercies."

His face crumpled. "Oh, really? I mean, are you sure?"

"Yes, Harley, that was the plan. You have to keep your hand in, the label wants to hear some new stuff soon, and Miss Nina here needs her routine."

"You don't think it's too early?"

"Seriously? No, God. You two have been joined at the hip for months, now get out of here. Cut the apron strings, push her out the nest, she needs to be a strong independent woman, and all that jazz."

"She's not even three months old."

"Yes, and I'm being sarcastic, jeez," said Rose. "I'm not actually going to teach your child how to balance her chequebook and get a mortgage while you're gone. You'll still have your baby girl when you get back."

"I don't even know how to balance a chequebook," Max piped up.

"Yeah, me neither," she said, shrugging. "Harley'll have to teach us how to adult later."

"It's an outdated expression," he said, distracted. "That's not important. Are you sure you're okay with her?"

"You'll be two hours, right?" Max asked. "Then, yeah, we'll be fine. Ignore Rose, she's being daft and not helping."

"Your face is daft," Rose muttered.

"But trust us. We promise to follow the instructions you've left us, and we'll call you if there's anything we can't handle. You can do this, Harley," he said, squeezing his shoulder and gazing intently into his eyes. "You are the chosen one."

Harley shook his head and narrowed his eyes. "You two are made for each other, you know that, right?"

Rose blushed fiercely and ducked her head. Luckily, Harley was too busy covering Nina's face with kisses to notice. Eventually, they got him out the door, and Rose leaned against it with a huff, looking up at Max. "Well, that's him gone. Let's swap all his sugar for salt and put his teabags in all sorts of weird places."

Max smirked and walked back into the sitting room with Nina. "You wouldn't. He's too knackered to notice, and you can't deprive a new parent of their hard-earned caffeine."

"You're no fun."

He carefully manoevered Nina off his shoulder and into his hands, crouching to put her onto a playmat. "What do we do with her now?" he asked as Nina looked up at the dangling toys and batted at a purple fish.

Rose scanned the detailed instructions Harley had left on the table and shrugged. "Bottle of milk in half an hour. I guess we, uh, what do people *do* with babies?"

He snorted. "Beats me. You're the one who produced her."

"Yeah, under duress," she added, coming to sit cross-legged next to him to stare at Nina, who was making some quite cute cooing noises.

"You don't regret it, then?" he asked softly.

She looked up sharply. He was focused on Nina's waving feet, and she gave in to the impulse to move closer and slip her hand onto his knee, an impulse she would have shot down not so long ago. "Not at all."

"Not even when she's so cute?"

She froze. "You don't…want one, do you?"

"Me? Oh God, no. I've never considered kids of my own. I mean, apart from the whole logistical nightmare. I mean, I know I'm young, all things considered, but I can't imagine it." He shifted and slipped his fingers into hers. "You know, Jamie's wanted kids for ages, too. Not right away, but he's hoping that if he ever meets a nice guy and wants to settle down that they'll adopt enough sprogs to fill that house, carry on the family name, you know? His sister's got kids, and he loves them, but he wants his own." He shook his head. "I never felt like that."

She nodded, letting out a long breath in relief. "I know. I mean, look at her, she's adorable. She's definitely the cutest baby I've ever seen, and she's so chill as well."

"Yeah, don't speak too soon. You'll jinx it, and she'll scream the rest of the time."

"Sorry, sorry, touch wood," she said, tapping Max's head. He pushed her off with a snort. "But I mean, if I can't summon up the maternal instinct for my own genetic progeny, who also happens to be extremely nice for a baby, then really, there's no hope for me. It's just proven what I already know. I do not want kids."

He nodded and leaned against her, some tension in his shoulders draining out. "You know," she said thoughtfully. "I can't imagine being like the other NCT mums. I can't even comprehend their thought process, can't relate to them at all. Nadine, the architect, you remember I mentioned her?" Max nodded. "Yeah, well, we used to chat loads before we had the babies. I thought I'd keep in touch with her for sure but since she had Alexis, it's like she's taken this massive, ten-mile step to the left, and I missed out somehow. She said she can't even really remember what she felt like as a person before she had him, and that scares the crap out of me, honestly. Like, what else changes your entire identity so completely?"

He shrugged. "Transitioning was pretty huge for me, obviously, but I don't know if that sounds the same. To me it was more like…I felt like me for the first time, rather than being hidden inside a shell that was too small for me and the wrong shape. But in terms of my identity, that didn't really change. I'd always been Max. It just took a while for other people to accept that."

She squeezed his arm tightly. "They were idiots. Max is awesome."

He leaned his face against her hair. "Do you think just Max is enough for you, though?" he asked softly.

She pulled back and cupped his cheek with one hand, the other still tangled up on his knee. "There's no such thing as *just* Max," she said, kissing him gently. "You're more than enough for me."

About the Author

Lyn Hemphill is Kenyan born and bred but now lives in Oxfordshire with her partner and two children, who like to help her come up with some more outlandish plot points. She writes every spare moment she can find, in between teaching science online and developing screenplays with her writing partner Aloïs Castel.

Books Available From Bold Strokes Books

Fleur d'Lies by MJ Williamz. For rookie cop DJ Sander, being true to what you believe is the only way to live...and one way to die. (978-1-63555-854-8)

Guarding Evelyn by Erin Zak. Can TV actress Evelyn Glass prove her love for Alden Ryan means more to her than fame before it's too late? (978-1-63555-841-8)

Love's Falling Star by B.D. Grayson. For country music megastar Lochlan Paige, can love conquer her fear of losing the one thing she's worked so hard to protect? (978-1-63555-873-9)

Love's Truth by C.A. Popovich. Can Lynette and Barb make love work when unhealed wounds of betrayed trust and a secret could change everything? (978-1-63555-755-8)

Next Exit Home by Dena Blake. Home may be where the heart is, but for Harper Sims and Addison Foster, is the journey back worth the pain? (978-1-63555-727-5)

Not Broken by Lyn Hemphill. Falling in love is hard enough—even more so for Rose, who's carrying her ex's baby. (978-1-63555-869-2)

The Noble and the Nightingale by Barbara Ann Wright. Two women on opposite sides of empires at war risk all for a chance at love. (978-1-63555-812-8)

What a Tangled Web by Melissa Brayden. Clementine Monroe has the chance to buy the café she's managed for years, but Madison LeGrange swoops in and buys it first. Now Clementine is forced to work for the enemy and ignore her former crush. (978-1-63555-749-7)

A Far Better Thing by JD Wilburn. When needs of her family and wants of her heart clash, Cass Halliburton is faced with the ultimate sacrifice. (978-1-63555-834-0)

Body Language by Renee Roman. When Mika offers to provide Jen erotic tutoring, will sex drive them into a deeper relationship or tear them apart? (978-1-63555-800-5)

Carrie and Hope by Joy Argento. For Carrie and Hope, loss brings them together but secrets and fear may tear them apart. (978-1-63555-827-2)

Detour to Love by Amanda Radley. Celia Scott and Lily Andersen are seatmates on a flight to Tokyo and by turns annoy and fascinate each other. But they're about to realize there's more than one path to love. (978-1-63555-958-3)

Ice Queen by Gun Brooke. School counselor Aislin Kennedy wants to help standoffish CEO Susanna Durr and her troubled teenage daughter become closer—even if it means risking her own heart in the process. (978-1-63555-721-3)

Masquerade by Anne Shade. In 1925 Harlem, New York, a notorious gangster sets her sights on seducing Celine, and new lovers Dinah and Celine are forced to risk their hearts, and lives, for love. (978-1-63555-831-9)

Royal Family by Jenny Frame. Loss has defined both Clay's and Katya's lives, but guarding their hearts may prove to be the biggest heartbreak of all. (978-1-63555-745-9)

Share the Moon by Toni Logan. Three best friends, an inherited vineyard, and a resident ghost come together for fun, romance, and a touch of magic. (978-1-63555-844-9)

Spirit of the Law by Carsen Taite. Attorney Owen Lassiter will do almost anything to put a murderer behind bars, but can she get past her reluctance to rely on unconventional help from the alluring Summer Byrne and keep from falling in love in the process? (978-1-63555-766-4)

The Devil Incarnate by Ali Vali. Cain Casey has so much to live for, but enemies who lurk in the shadows threaten to unravel it all. (978-1-63555-534-9)

Secret Agent by Michelle Larkin. CIA Agent Peyton North embarks on a global chase to apprehend rogue agent Zoey Blackwood, but her commitment to the mission is tested as the sparks between them ignite and their sizzling attraction approaches a point of no return. (978-1-63555-753-4)